"Viking Worlds, Book I" is a collection of historical occurrences and important events of the Nordic world which are brought to life again through the imagination of the author. It tells the story of how the Norwegian Rollo founded Normandy, or how a proselytizing priest caused trouble in Iceland. It tells of the young Greenlander Leif Eriksson who, following a legend, discovered the continent now known as America five hundred years prior to Columbus. It recounts the life of the Pagan Viking King Olaf who became a devout Christian, and attempted to unite his country in the new faith.

Rainer W. Grimm was born in September 1964, as the son of a coalminer. His hometown is Gelsenkirchen which lies in Northrhine-Westfalia, Germany. Being unable to perform his two studied trades after a back injury, he started writing historical novels and stories as an indipendent author. His first publication in german language was the three volume Saga of Eric Sigurdsson, followed by the novel "Pact of the Barbarians", which concerns itself with the Battle of the Teutoburg Forest and the Roman Empire`s campaigns in Germania. Then he published the two volume Saga of Sigurd Svensson and the three Books of the Viking World Series.

Rainer W. Grimm

*

VIKING WORLDS
BOOK 1

Historical Occurrences and Important Events from
the World of the Vikings

*

Translated by
Phillip Michael Cowden

Bibliografische Information Der Deutschen Bibliothek:
*Die Deutsche Bibliothek verzeichnet diese Publikation in der
Deutschen Nationalbibliografie; detaillierte bibliografische Daten
sind im Internet über* http://dnb.ddb.de *abrufbar.*

All rights reserved
© Rainer W. Grimm, 2017 (first published German version 2009)
www.authorrainerwgrimm.jimdo.com
Herstellung und Verlag: Books on Demand GmbH,
Norderstedt
Printed in Germany
Titelgestaltung, Layout: RWG&DG
ISBN: 978-3-7431-0110-4

MIX
Papier aus verantwortungsvollen Quellen
Paper from responsible sources
FSC® C105338

CONTENTS

1. THE ATTACK ON LINDISFARNE 11
2. ROLLO AND THE TOPPLED KING 13
3. THE SAGA OF OLAF TRYGGVESSON ... 25
4. THANGBRAND THE MISSIONARY 65
5. THE NEW WORLD 71
6. ALFRED THE GREAT 95
7. THE BATTLE OF HJÖRUNGAFJORD ... 109

*

1. The Attack of Lindisfarne

I am called Alcuin the Priest and I was once a devoted missionary! Yes, I was a diligent servant of the Lord Jesus Christ and even a counsel to Charlemagne, the great King of the Franks. But now I have become an old man of seventy three years, and by the light of a candle I hold my quill with a trembling hand to record what happened less than a decade ago.

I know, for I was there! Fate had led me in my old age away from the realm of the Franks and back to my home of Northumberland in beautiful Britain. In the rich abbey of Lindisfarne, located on the island of the same name off the north eastern coast of my native country, I found sanctuary and was welcomed most warmly by the abbot of the monastery. Here in this house beloved by God, here where our Saints Cuthbert and Aidan had lived, did I wish to find peace to prepare myself for the journey to the Kingdom of Heaven of Almighty God. It pleased the Lord, however, to show me once more, man's capacity for cruelty and barbarity. I had already seen the many abominations that the victors of a battle are wont to commit in the retinue of Charlemagne. Even kings and lords such as Carolus Rex (or perhaps they in particular) were inclined to enslave the vanquished, if not outright kill them in their thousands. There is little of the love that our Lord Jesus Christ preached in their deeds, and only seldom did they show mercy towards the peoples they conquered. But even worse were those who acted out of greed. They killed, raped and ransacked purely out of avarice. Godless barbarians were they!

During the spring, great storms raged over the land of Northumbria. Dragons appeared in the darkened sky spouting fire. These were all portents that something terrible was about to occur. No, it would not be a good year! And so it happened on the 8th of June anno Domini 793, and never before had anything worse befallen us. The blood of priests stained the walls and floor of the church of St. Cuthbert. Indeed, this was the beginning of all sorrows.

The monastery sat on a hill with a beautiful view of the bay. Rich green meadows upon which bright colorful flowers and only a few gnarled old trees grew reached down to the strand. It was the time of the morning prayer when the angular sails of two longships appeared on the horizon. And the sips of the godless vikings were headed for our bay. A young novice by the name of Ambrose was the first to be struck down by the Northmen's blades. It was said that this Ambrose was at the beach that morning to disport himself with a girl from a nearby village. That may well have been so, for later, the lifeless body of a young woman was found not far from the unfortunate one's own corpse.
The Northmen violated the luckless maid extensively before relieving her of her earthly torment, and there were those monks in the monastery who saw this as the Lord's just punishment. I on the other hand mourn for those poor souls, for I know that many women of that area spread their legs for the brothers for a bit of food or coin. Let he who is without sin cast the first stone.
Then the heathens stormed up the meadow and towards the abbey enclosed merely by a low wall offering little protection. Fair was the hair flowing beneath the iron helms of the tall men, and long were their beards. With blades held high, swinging axes over their heads, the pagans assaulted

the church doors. Only now did the bell sound to warn the brothers of the danger, but it was far too late!
The lock of the great wooden gate was broken and the doors crashed against the walls allowing the heathen barbarians to storm the house of God. They shouted the word "Viking" again and again, and they descended upon the praying and fearfully screaming monks like wild animals. The brothers ran in panic through the church hall, confused and weeping, and many were struck down by the axes of the hellish brood. The abbot who confronted the bloodthirsty savages cross in hand had his skull split to the root of the nose by the sharp and heavy blade of a sword. The monks cried out in shock and fear and attempted to flee but only few were able to escape the church. Most of them, however, shared in the fate of the abbot and stood before the face of our Creator that dreadful day. Then the murderers gathered together everything of value. They took the golden vessels for the blessed Eucharist and the crosses made of silver. The monks' rings and pectorals they tore from their lifeless bodies.
I myself was in my bed in a room inside the main abbey building during all this. I was after all sixty three years of age and no longer in good health. God alone knows why he spared this old monk's life. It was one of the novices who came storming into my chamber under the roof crying out in utmost distress "The vikings are coming! The vikings are coming!"
But what could an old man possibly do? I remained upon my straw filled mattress and folded my hands in prayer to my God that he be merciful to me in death. Then my door was burst open. The vikings had now also taken the main building and were searching every nook and cranny for valuables, killing everyone in their path. Frozen in fear, as I must shamefully confess, I lay there as the door was torn

from its hinges and a tall strongly fellow entered the dimly lit chamber. He looked around briefly then approached my bed sword drawn. Now the moment has come, where I will meet my Creator, I thought to myself. But to my surprise the viking's blade did not pierce my body. I dared to tentatively open my eyes which I had firmly shut. The man stood there for a moment, looking down at this old body. Bright, indeed blazing blue eyes stared at me and I looked back at an almost boyish face framed by a closely cropped blonde beard. This man had seen no more than twenty summers, yet heaven alone knew how many people he had brought to death. Should he be the one to end my long life? So I lay there, staring into the blue eyes of this youth, waiting for his blade to fall. But suddenly the viking spoke to me. I did not understand his words, of course, but his voice was calm, almost peaceful. Then he smiled and left my room. Oh Lord, what encounter was this? While my brothers were begging for their lives and being slaughtered, I experienced this miracle of clemency. I, an old man who had already lived his life. Now I slowly rose, for I no longer felt the pains of my ailments. I hesitantly went over to the chamber's small window and saw the Northmen beladen with the treasures of the monastery, with our food and livestock, crossing the meadow back down to the shore. And it was of the greatest ignominy that they sang merrily as they went.

As swiftly as they had come, they were gone again. But the name they had called still echoed in the ears of the survivors long after. With impunity and without losing a single one of theirs, the thieves were on their way. For many long years I stood at the side of Charlemagne, witnessed wars and men dying for their faith. Yet such a blow, swift and without mercy, I had never before seen in my life.

Slowly I descended down the stairs and looked upon the harm these bloodthirsty savages had caused. Many of the brothers were lying in their own blood, and the church of St. Cuthbert was in flames.

The monks and novices who dared come out of hiding tended to the wounded. Others ran like headless fowl with pales of water across the church square, but only after help from the nearby village arrived could the old church be saved from the flames.

What baseness! What a disgrace for Christendom! Never in all the long years that we and our forefathers have settled in this fair land has there been such an attack on Britain as the one by these barbaric pagans we were forced to witness. Who would have thought such an attack from the sea possible?

This, however, was only the prelude to these sorrowful times! For only one year later the Northmen returned to gorge themselves on a our beloved homeland.

The abbeys of Monkwearmouth and Jarrow were their ambition and they suffered no lesser cruelties than we at Lindisfarne had one year earlier.

In the year 795 the news was spread across all the realms of the British Isles that the Vikings had sacked the Island of Iona in Scotland. And not long ago the Isle of Man suffered the same fate.

I, Alcuin, who is known as the Frank, old and marked by death, I beseech you, Lord Jesus Christ, have mercy on your children. Have mercy, in the face of the doom these vikings, who worship the devil Odin, may yet bring to us!

*

2. Rollo and the Toppled King

I will tell you the saga of Göngu Hrolf, of Rolf the Vagabond! It was during the time when King Harald Harfagr, whom all called Harald Fairhair, reigned over the land on the North Way. There, in a fjord far in the north of the country, lived a young farmer named Rolf, though all called him Rollo. This man was loved but little among his neighbors, for he was considered unfriendly and very violent. Often, Rollo would quarrel with the other farmers, and many times the local lord would be forced to restore order at the *thing*[1]. And so it came to pass that the belligerent farmer was once more called before the lord of Helgeland, but this time, it did not look good for him. A neighbor's sheep had grazed on Rollo's meadows. This had enraged the short-tempered man to such a degree, he wasted no time and slew his neighbor in anger. Now accused of manslaughter, Rollo was lead again to the lord of Helgeland. But being stubborn and headstrong, Rollo refused to pay a weregild[2]. After all, it was the neighbor's own fault, he thought. But the *jarl*[3] and the elders had enough of his cheek, and without further ado they banished the hot-tempered farmer to the Orkney Isles for four years and forbade him return to his home land on pain of death.

But only two years did the exile stay on the Orkneys, for then he readied his ship to sail the Northern Sea. As time

---

1 Germanic governing assembly, Old English spelling "Þing", cf. Anglo-Saxon "folkmoot".
2 "Man price": a fine to be paid when injuring or killing a person.
3 Chieftain, Scandinavian word for "earl".

went by, more and more warriors joined and soon he commanded a fully manned *snekja*[4] with which he raided the coasts of Norway as a pirate and viking. Thus the farmer who was banished to the Orkney Isles made an evil name for himself in the Nordic Kingdoms. Many sea-kings sought his allegiance, and so it came to pass that Rolf, whom the folk of the north now called the Vagabond, swore fealty to a Danish viking lord. No coast was safe from the viking fleet of this Danish sea-king, and no army could stop their raids. The lands of the Saxons, the great trading ports of the Frisians, the cities on the rivers of the realm of Poland, and the island of the Anglo-Saxons were all ravaged and ransacked. The Dane spared the coasts of the Northlands, however, which vexed Rollo greatly, for he desired to return to Helgeland: for revenge!
But he had to follow his king's orders, for he had sworn an oath; and breaking that oath would not have been wise. With each passing raid, however, the discontent among the vikings grew. They were displeased with the unequal sharing of the spoils. The sea-king paid his followers poorly and kept the larger part of the treasures for himself. And so it was Rollo, who raised his voice and instigated the mutiny against their Danish leader.

When he knew enough of the warriors were on his side, he stood before the viking lord and spoke threateningly.
"For too long now, have you cheated us out of our fair portion, Dane! It is time for a more honest man to take your place!"
"And this man would be you, Rollo?", the sea-king hissed quietly, and then laughed bitterly.
"I know not, whether I be the man to take your place, But I know I will be the one to ram his iron into your hide!"

---

4 Fast viking sailing ship with 30 oars.

The larger part of the warriors began to cheer, but their were some men who were much less enthused, and some even yet loyal to their chief. Rollo drew his sword and the Dane did likewise.

"Now you will pay for your cheek, Rollo!", the viking chief cried. The Norwegian swung his sword at the sea-king in answer. The blades clashed together loudly, and the men cheered at every blow of one or the other warrior. Rollo was the younger of the combatants, having seen around twenty-seven summers and winters. His Danish opponent on the other hand had already celebrated the midsummer feast more than forty times. But the viking chief was an experienced and skilled warrior and did not go easy on Rollo. And yet, the longer the battle raged on, the more the Norwegian's will to triumph grew, and the Dane's sword arm was growing heavier. Every blow and thrust with the iron weapons wore on the men, and so the younger was soon at an advantage. Still it was Rollo who received the first wound, for a quick slash had struck his face and cut his cheek. Not a deep cut, but painful. And now his ire, for which he had been exiled from Helgeland in the first place, burst forth. With no regard for his own life, he hacked at the Danish sea-king. Stroke for stroke his sword swung down on his opponent, and before long Rolf's iron had found its mark. A blow struck the chief in the shoulder, ripping through his leather jerkin, and the blood gushing forth from the deep wound soon drenched the Dane's woolen shirt. But the man would not give up. With the courage born of desperation, he attacked Rollo once more, but his strength had left him, and now, it was child's play for Rollo the Vagabond. He drove his blade straight through his chest with a sickening crack, as the steel pierced the breastbone. The Dane succumbed to his terrible injuries shortly after, and the men chose Rollo to be his successor. Thus, an exiled

Norwegian farmer became a sea-king with a fleet of five ships and an army comprised mainly of Danish warriors. And so the viking Rollo attacked the coasts of Norway, Sweden and Denmark, as was his wont and to still his thirst for revenge. Revenge for the dishonor of being banished. The sea-king raided many a settlement, and now that he had a fleet at his command, even the larger cities were not safe from him. Soon there was not a king in all of Thule[5], who would not try to get rid of this scourge.

It was already autumn and heavy storms roared across the northern sea. Few traders and warriors dared to cross the angry waters in their ships.
"Yes, now is the right time come to attack a great city!", thought Rollo. For during the autumn and approaching winter the people of the North thought themselves secure, and they slacked in their watchfulness. They would have much to plunder, for the coffers of the *hersir*[6] and money chests of the rich traders were often well filled after summer. And it was also the time when the tax collectors of the kings traveled through the land to collect the tithe. Ignoring the misgivings of some of his more seasoned warriors, the viking king made ready his ships.

The sky was gray and heavy rain poured down on the men as they rowed out from their hiding place, a small island in a fjord not far from the Shetlands. A strong wind blew from the north and filled the strained sails almost to the point of tearing. The southern coast of Norway would be their target for here were many rich towns that profited from the trade with the merchants of the realms of the Germans, the Franks

---

5 Old term for the Scandinavian kingdoms.
6 Local viking military commander, leader of a "hundred" (county subdivision) owing allegiance to a king or Jarl

and the Poles. The jarls and hersir of the southern regions even allowed the Christian priests to spread their religion and many towns already had a church. This, in turn, had drawn the rich traders of the south to the places of commerce in the north. But as Rollo the sea-king came to Hardanger to raid the town of Lindesnes, he found an unpleasant surprise waiting for him. The news of an approaching army of vikings had spread quickly, and so Rollo was already expected at Hardanger. The might of the ruling jarl by the name of Erik was great, for he was the eldest son of the Norwegian king Harald Fairhair, and he would later receive the name "Bloodaxe" for the murder of his brothers in their struggle for power. The element of surprise was no longer on the side of the pirates, for the jarl of Hardanger had sent an army to Lindesnes to throw the vikings back into the stormy sea.

When Rollo saw the vast contingent of ships arrayed against him off the coast of the great trading town, he gave the order to turn the snekja around and sail out to sea again. But now the viking fleet was caught in a fierce autumn storm and was blown south. Some of the men thought that the sea-king had fallen from grace and that the gods were angrily punishing him for attacking his own folk out of revenge. But still they followed him.

After a good while, they came out of the storm, and it was their good fortune that the ships had not taken much damage, and to the amazement of his men, Rollo ordered them to sail further south. And so the five tall ships of the northmen reached the western coast of Francia. They rowed inland up a river until presently they came upon a spot to their leader's liking. Here the men made landfall, pulled their ships onto the beach and erected a large fortified camp. And they promptly started to attack the surrounding villages and settlements. They stole the livestock, raped the women and killed the men. By the onset of winter, all the settlements and farms near the viking encampment had been abandoned and the folk there had fled. But to Rollo the Sea-King's astonishment, the invaders were left largely unhindered. No army came to confront the vikings and punish them for their deeds. What a coward the ruler of this country must be! Rollo thought wintering here a good idea, for they had food and water, a warm fire and slave women. Furthermore wood in abundance, and so over time their tents became huts. Soon they even built great longhouses, and Rollo, being their leader and sea-king, had the finest. They even built a great mead hall in which the vikings celebrated. Some of the Frankish women they had caught had become their brides, and it seemed almost as if the mob of savage vikings had become a group of simple settlers.

But the peace ended with the coming of spring, for Rollo would not become a simple farmer again. He was still the same unruly viking who had fled the Orkneys several winters ago, and now, with the snow melting, he wished to see what else this realm of the Franks had to offer a wild Northman. Rollo had often heard of the wealthy cities along the river which the Franks called the Seine, and now he would see, what truth there was to those stories. After all, he wouldn't be the first viking to sail to the gates of Paris. During the winter they had mended their ships and now, watered and victualed, they loaded their possessions onto them and cast off to find plunder. Only a handful of men were left behind to guard the camp.

The dragon ships sailed up the great river, following its course southwards. And soon they came upon a small town where the Northmen would test their mettle. At the crack of dawn, while the town was still half asleep, the keels of the boats glided up onto the sand of the riverbank, and the attack began. The town's guards could not withstand the Vikings and were slaughtered in short order. But many of the townsmen were hardy and gave the Vikings battle, so the raid was restricted to that quarter of the town closest to the river. But soon the incident was over, for as quickly as they had come, the vikings left again.

They made camp at a convenient location downstream to see how much they had stolen, but it turned out to be far less than what the men had hoped for. Since Rollo and his warriors were unable to reach the town center, the house of the hersir with all its treasures as well as the town's coffers had eluded them. Angrily, Rollo was forced to acknowledge that his army was too small to successfully attack a city. So they roamed the countryside and raided farms and villages and occasionally the seat of a count. And the longer Rollo and his Vikings raided the north of Francia, the louder the folk there cried out for vengeance.

But whenever the Frankish king sent out an army to do battle with the Northmen, they would be long gone. The Vikings played this game of cat-and-mouse all throughout the summer until the first colored leaves of autumn fell, and they returned to their encampment in the north of the country.

Their ships were filled with the plunder of the last summer when their keels touched the beach near their camp at the Seine. They were greeted warmly by their fellows who had waited long for their return. Many a Viking had become a father during the summer and was astonished when the Frankish woman he had left so many months ago put a baby in his arms. Autumn was rapidly approaching and leaves were falling from the trees in heaps. It was getting markedly colder, but not nearly as cold as in their homeland, and so the Northmen felt quite comfortable in their settlement.

Some of them had even moved into the surrounding abandoned farms and started leading the normal lives of farmers. And even more men came to the settlement to join the Viking king Rollo. They had sailed from Denmark to Francia after hearing of Rollo's conquest and the beauty of the land.

But the tide would turn! It was the winter of the year 911 AD and the first snow had fallen, when a great Frankish army closed in on the area Rollo had seized for himself. The Viking King promptly assembled his warriors and marched against the Franks. When the armies met a great battle ensued and the Frankish King, Charles III, overpowered the unwanted invaders. The ruler so often mocked as cowardly by the Viking king hat forced the army of the Norwegian to its knees. And so the proud Nordic warriors were forced to acknowledge defeat. But before the Viking king could fall upon his sword in grief, Charles had him brought before his thrown.
"You and your Northmen have harmed my country greatly", he spoke grimly. "But you shall receive the opportunity to make reparations for your deeds."
The Viking looked at King Charles in surprise, as he had thought he would now lose his head. But the king stood up and said: "Every year murdering and plundering Viking hordes like yourself invade my country and torment my people! This costs me greatly in warriors throughout the years!"
The king's gaze was strict, but he did not speak in anger. "You, Rollo, will be the one to put a stop to your own kind!"
Rollo, not understanding, stared at the king with surprise.
"You and your army of Northmen will keep these robbers in check! In exchange you may live unmolested on those lands

that you have already taken!" Rollo could not believe what he was hearing. Instead of giving him his death sentence, this king was asking for his fealty. "And what if I refuse?", the Norwegian asked boldly.

The king raised his eyebrows, amazed at such audacity. "Then you will lose your head this very day, and every last one of your men along with you! Your houses will burn and your wives and your bastards will die! If I have been informed correctly, then you Northmen must die an honorable warrior's death with sword in hand in order to be called before your gods. Is this not true?", the Frank slyly asked and turned to his bishop. "What barbaric superstition", he said snidely, and the bishop nodded in agreement. "Your end will be less than honorable, Rollo!", Charles said loudly so that all could hear. It would not be an honorable death and the gods would surely deny him and his followers entry into Valhalla, the Viking king thought to himself. And yet Rollo was not too quick to bind himself by oath to a foreign lord, and he justified his hesitation by stating that he must consult with his men first. Now it was the turn of the Frankish king to look amazed.

"I thought you were their leader", he asked in surprise.

"That is true King Charles. But I was freely chosen by the men! As they gave me leadership, so can they take it from me again", Rollo explained.

"Fine, so be it! I will give you time for consideration" the king said graciously, and let Rollo return to his settlement unharmed. But the Vikings' five ships the king took back to his capital. They would be returned after accepting his offer. If they refused, they wouldn't be needing them anymore. Those were the words of parting the Frankish king spoke with a smug smile.

The King of the Franks held the Northmen captive in his country for a full year, and Rollo defiantly kept him waiting. But the Norwegian's men had become settled. They had farms and families they did not wish to lose. Some had even converted to the Christian faith in secret. Finally Charles III summoned Rollo to his seat of power and offered him contract. The Norwegian and all of his followers would be baptized, and Rollo would repel Viking invasions as a vassal of the Frankish king. In exchange, he would receive the lands on the lower Seine where he had erected his settlement as a fief. The men of the North assembled at the *thing* and agreed to the terms.

And so King Charles summoned Rollo to place called Saint-Claire-sur-Epte. There the signing of the treaty was to be made official and to be properly celebrated, of course. Rollo the Viking and his captains were ordered before the king. So the former sea-king arrived with a score of men as his retinue to finally submit to the Frankish king. The king had also invited all of the Frankish nobility to the celebration, so that the whole court could see that he, Charles III, had vanquished the savage Viking Rollo. The Northmen were greeted warmly and led into ostentatious chambers in which they were to wait until summoned by the king. The treaty between the ruler of Francia and Rollo, the Viking king, was to be signed today. But in the evening, when the festivities commenced, an unpleasant surprise awaited the Northmen. The Frank made a fiery speech and the noblemen hung on his every word, as if they were made of pure gold. Every now and again the king would be interrupted by thunderous applause, until his speech finally ended. Then suddenly all stared at Rollo the Viking. The great hall had become so quiet, one could have heard a pin dropping. The Northmen looked at one another questioningly for they knew not, what was happening. Had they been lured into deadly trap after all? Would they now be slaughtered for the amusement of the present guests? But then a footman appeared before the leader of the Vikings.

"My lord, it is customary in our land to kiss the foot of one's liege lord", he whispered softly.

"What?" Rollo burst out loudly. And immediately the other Northmen wished to know, what the lackey had said. And when they had heard, they too erupted in outrage at such an honorless request.

"Never!", the once so feared sea king cried out, and bristled at the thought of this duty. He was warrior to be feared after all, not a servant, he rumbled loudly into the hall so that all could hear. There was an uproar as the Frankish nobility was distraught and outraged that the Northman would refuse to bow his head to the king. Some demanded loudly that the Vikings be driven out of the land by force of arms. But King Charles remained calm and commanded the court to be silent.

Rollo too, wanted to avoid fighting, for the Frank's offer appealed to him greatly. And so he simply ordered one of his captains to kiss the king's foot in his stead. A man named Gunnar with the byname Broadnose was chosen. This Gunnar Broadnose was a stately warrior and he had long been loyal to Rollo. He was a Norwegian, like his leader, and had raided with him since they had left the Orkney Isles. But even loyal Gunnar saw this order as an insult. Rollo persuaded the proud Viking that it would be an honor to stand before the King of the Franks in his stead, a true and unalterable act of friendship, and so grumbling, Gunnar agreed. Somewhat hesitantly the two men stepped up to the Frankish king, but Gunnar was not willing to throw himself to the floor in front of this ruler. So he quickly grabbed Charles's III foot and raised it up so he could kiss it without stooping down too much. Slowly, bit by bit, the king leaned back, until he finally fell backwards off his chair. The Frankish ladies screamed in horror, as they saw their king lying there. The men of the court were no less appalled. The delegation of Vikings however burst out in laughter, and some of the attendants thought that that surely would be the end of them now. Armed warriors with helms and colorful surcoats stormed the hall, ready to fall upon the Vikings. But the "toppled" king held them back. Charles III, King of Francia, quizzically shook his head and began to laugh himself. Great merriment soon entered the hall and riotous celebrations ensued. Charles, King of the Franks, was not only a humorous man, but also wise and was gifted with far-sightedness. For it did indeed turn out that he had found a strong and above all loyal liegeman in Rollo, who would drive out any Viking invaders, just as the king had hoped. Rollo was granted the title of count of Rouen, and the Franks called the land that he ruled henceforth Normandy!

*

3. The Saga of Olaf Tryggvesson

In the time when Harald Harfagr who was known as Fairhair was the sole ruler of Norway, and he had proclaimed his son Erik his successor, conflict arose between Harald's sons.
Without pity, Erik killed two of his brothers by the names of Rögnvald and Björn.
And his other brothers by the names of Sigröd and Olaf were defeated by him in a great battle. But their sons and heirs, called Godröd and Tryggve, managed to escape their murderous kin. Yet now their lives were in the utmost of danger, as their uncle passionately wished for their deaths. For by right of birth they had a claim to the throne, which Erik claimed for himself.

Hakon, the youngest of the Haraldsons, had been raised in the lands of the Saxons. With the help of the Saxon king Aethelstan, he drove his brother Erik, who by now held the byname "Bloodaxe", out of his domain. And in the areas of Vingulmark and Ranrike, he installed his nephew Tryggve as a petty king, Godröd received Hardanger as a fief.
But the blood feud between the offspring of the great king Harald Fairhair continued. For soon afterwards, Hakon the Good was defeated and killed in battle by Harald Eriksson, the oldest son of Erik Bloodaxe. But as Harald was a vassal of the Danish king, and only with his help did he accomplish this deed, petty king Tryggve Olafsson denied him the oath of fealty.

But with a cunning ruse, King Harald was able to set a trap for the unruly Tryggve and kill him. And so Queen Astrid, the wife of Tryggve, and her two daughters fled the royal city of Sotenäset to the uplands of Norway to her parents' home. And during her flight she gave birth to a son, whom she named Olaf, as was the custom.

Thorbart, the loyal companion of Astrid, who had come to the court of the petty king Tryggve as a slave many summers ago, and was a Briton by birth, firmly believed in salvation through the Lord Christ. He took the child and sprinkled it with water.

"I baptize you, Olaf, in the name of the Father, and the Son, and the Holy Ghost", he spoke and made the sign of the Cross over the child's head, "May the Lord Jesus Christ keep you safe."

And so Olaf was baptized for the first time, without him ever realizing. But soon it became clear that the queen was not safe even in the home of her parents, for Harald Eriksson had heard of the birth of the heir of King Tryggve, and now sought to kill the boy.

Hounded by Harald's men, Queen Astrid and her son fled to Sweden. Her daughters she left with her parents for they were in less danger, having no claim to the throne. Astrid wished to travel on from Sweden to Holmgard[7] to her brother Sigurd.

Now this Sigurd was a liegeman to Grand Prince Vladimir of Kiev and a great captain of men. She would be safe from Harald's harassment with him. Accompanied by her old foster father Thorbart and his son Thorstein, she embarked on the perilous journey. But on the long voyage across the Warangian Sea their ship was attacked by Estonian pirates, and the erstwhile Queen Astrid and her little son were forced to endure slavery. Loyal Thorbart was slain, and his son, six years Olaf's senior, shared the fate of the enslaved. At this time Olaf was three years of age.

---

7 Nordic name for Novgorod.

Seven years passed during which Olaf Tryggvesson and Thorstein were thralls to a farmer in Livonia. Former queen Astrid had been separated from her child in hot bitter tears at the slave market, for she had been sold to another slave holder. And so time passed. Thorstein in the mean time had reached a trusted position on the farm because of his honesty and mercantile skills, he was allowed to sell the farmer's wares at the market in the trading town of Daugmale.

The farmer knew he could trust Thorstein, for he knew the young lad would never attempt to escape without his brotherly friend Olaf. And that was indeed true, for Thorstein and Astrid's son were inseparable. Countless times, the son of Thorbart had told young Olaf of his uncle, the Jarl Sigurd, and so they remained hopeful that one day they would yet escape slavery.

And so it came to pass that one day the tax collector of the Grand Prince of Kiev came to Daugmale and visited the market. Thorstein coincidentally overheard the warriors calling their leader Jarl Sigurd. This man was a Norseman! Maybe even a Norwegian by birth, thought Thorstein. The brother of the queen who had gone to Holmgard had the same name. Could this be Astrid's sibling?

Risking mortal danger, Thorstein fell to his knees before the jarl, for a slave who dared address a high lord could consider himself lucky to only receive a flogging.

"My lord", he spoke quickly, "Are you the brother-in-law of King Tryggve?"

One of the warriors raised his sword to quiet the cheeky slave. But the jarl bade him sheath his blade. Astonished, he looked down at the young man with the closely shorn hair common for thralls.

"What did you just say, slave?"

Cold sweat stood in great drops on young Thorstein's brow and he scarcely dared breathe. "Jarl Sigurd, pardon my insolence and do not kill me for daring to speak to you", he stammered, "But it is a matter of life and death for your kin, if you are who I think you are!"

"What do you know of my kin?", the jarl asked angrily.

"Tell me first, whether you are the brother of Queen Astrid", Thorstein demanded, despite knowing that asking the lord this question could cost him his life. But the jarl nodded and Thorstein's heart nearly burst with joy. It was truly him! Now all sorrows would come to an end!

"I have tidings of one of your kin believed lost, Jarl", said Thorstein as he regained his composure. His hands steadied and his fear evaporated.

"You know of my missing sister Astrid?", the jarl asked, now visibly excited, "Go on, talk, boy!"

But the slave shook his head. "Alas, the fate of you sister, the queen is only known to me up to the day she was separated from her son Olaf and sold at the slave market. But I know where the son of King Tryggve and Queen Astrid is!"

"My sister's son is alive?", the jarl asked in visible astonishment. "Where does he live?"

"He shares my fate and lives as the slave of a farmer not far from Daugmale", Thorstein answered and told the jarl the entire story of their escape, as well as he could remember. In that same hour, the jarl let Thorstein lead him and his warriors to the farm, and when he saw the boy, he knew immediately that this was the son of Astrid.

"You are the son of King Tryggve and my sister", he exclaimed, "Yes, you are my nephew! Thank the gods!"

"Oh Sigurd, oh my uncle!", Olaf stuttered tearfully, and the kinsmen fell into one another's arms.

But now the farmer protested. This was after all his slave, and he was not willing to let him leave. Only after the threat of violence and proper payment did the farmer acquiesce. And brave Thorstein was also freed for Olaf borrowed the money from his uncle to pay for his beloved friend's release. Jarl Sigurd bought them both war gear with sword and dagger at the market of Daugmale as a sign of their freedom, and a few days later they sailed with Sigurd's fleet to Holmgard.

*

Olaf and Thorstein lived as members of Jarl Sigurd's household for almost a year. He lived in a great and stately house in Holmgard and had been married to the daughter of a rich Warangian[8] Merchant for nearly two years.
Olaf's mother-brother was a wealthy man and commanded great respect in the town.
Winter had already arrived, and one day the jarl was summoned to the palace of the Grand Prince; and while Olaf went to see his lord, Olaf and Thorstein were strolling through the large market place of Holmgard. All around them the merchants were loudly plying their wares. So too were the slavers.
"Strong, brawny fellows! Good for any manner of labor!", they shouted at the buyers. "Pretty women who know how to work by day and warm your bed by night!"
"Let us leave here", Olaf said, for he could not stand to look at the poor creatures. Too much did they remind him of his own fate, and the fate that his mother had endured.
"Wait a moment", Thorstein said, as he glared angrily at the slave trader upon the auction platform hawking his wares.

---

8 Warangian: Slavic name for Vikings

"No, come! What good could possibly come of this?", Olaf asked reproachfully.

"Look at that fellow up there", exclaimed Thorstein, now visibly excited, "You were likely too young and can't remember, but that scoundrel up there is the slaver who sold us into bondage!"

Young Olaf looked at his friend disbelievingly. "Are you sure? That was such a long time ago."

"I will never forget that voice for as long as I live. That man killed my father!", Thorstein proclaimed indignantly, "And I will never forget that ugly face!"

"If that is the man who killed your father, then he is also the one who sold my mother into slavery. For that, he will die by my sword", Olaf said with a firm voice.

"You cannot do this, Olaf! In the market he is protected by law!" Thorstein warned his friend, for he did not doubt that the boy would make good on his threat.

Yet it happened that same day, while Thorstein was not looking: With his dagger in hand, Olaf stood before the slaver, and his dying scream echoed across the market place, upon which the young lad fled from the angry merchants through the streets of Holmgard and to the house of Jarl Sigurd.

"Release the murderer unto us, Jarl!", they shouted threateningly. "He has broken the peace of the market and that is punishable by death! His life is forfeit!", the pursuers demanded furiously.

Then the jarl came to the door of his house with his sword drawn. "He who dares harm a hair on the head of my sister-son, I will cut to pieces! I swear it by Odin!"

But the mob would not be dissuaded and demanded Olaf's head. Now the jarl called for his warriors to assemble, for he knew the situation was dangerous.

"The Prince will pass judgment on this matter, and I recognize no authority but his!"

But only after help from the castle had arrived – for a captain had noticed the commotion and sent his guards to Sigurd's house - could they go the palace unmolested.

The anger of the Prince was great, and he was indeed willing to execute Olaf for slaying the merchant. Only the clemency of Grand Princess Rogeneta, the wife of Vladimir of Kiev, spared Olaf the gallows.

"You cannot send a child that avenged his mother to the executioner, my husband", she spoke, her mild voice full of emotion after hearing the story of Olaf Tryggvesson.

"Besides, he is the son of a king!"

For a moment the Prince pondered this irksome situation, shaking his head. But then his face lit up and he said with a sly expression "You're right, my dear wife. The laws regarding the peace of the market refer to men. This boy however is surely no older than ten summers. And no one may ask that I have children executed!

"Jarl Sigurd, you will pay an adequate weregild for the slain, and the child shall go free!"

The jarl thanked his lord and the gods of Valhalla and submitted to the judgment of his liege. But the Princess was so full of pity at the tale of the boy that she stroked his blonde hair and lovingly kissed him. Soon thereafter Grand Princess Rogeneta took young Olaf into her retinue, as he was of royal blood, and he served her as a page for a year. Thus he received a good education.

But at the age of twelve he followed his brotherly friend Thorstein and joined the army of the Grand Prince. Side by side with other sons of jarls and lords, the offspring of the Norwegian petty king Tryggve was instructed in all the arts of warfare, to later serve as a captain in the host of Vladimir.

In the campaigns against rebellious tribes, Olaf demonstrated his courage and skill time after time. And everyone knew that one day he would be a great captain.

Then it came to pass that one day Greek-orthodox missionaries came to Kiev to show the ruler the advantages of Christianity. The Greek monks knew all too well how to flatter the lord of Holmgard. They spoke of teaching the Russian boys how to read and write, the cornerstones of a good administration. They also offered the Greek secrets of architecture and medicine, if only the prince would be baptized and transform his land into a Christian realm. And they offered a pact with the East Roman emperor Basileios II, which would be of great benefit to Holmgard. And so Grand Prince Vladimir was not opposed to bowing to the customs of the East Roman Church.

At this time it so happened that the pagan inhabitants of the city of Chernigov attacked the few Christians of the city. Thorstein was captain of the guard there, and he loved the daughter of a wealthy Christian merchant, and had already secretly joined the followers of Jesus Christ. So when the pagans demanded the daughter of the merchant as a sacrifice for the god Frey, Thorstein openly sided with his future father-in-law.
Now there were several Greeks residing as guests in the keep of the Warangian merchant, and only one of them was able to escape, when the townsfolk attacked. He was forced to watch all the Christians of the town die horribly from the other side of the nearby river. Filled with rage, he traveled to Kiev to bitterly bemoan the deaths of his countrymen. Prince Vladimir was overcome with anger and ordered the entire city to be punished for this act of cruelty.

When Olaf heard of the death of his beloved friend he swore to take terrible revenge, and he was immediately offerd the opportunity. For the Prince sent him with many Warangian warriors to Chernigov to implement his sentence. The Prince of Holmgard's orders were obeyed without mercy. All the men were killed by Olaf Tryggveson's Warangians. The women and children were sold into slavery, the city itself was burned to the ground.

*

The pagan realm of Holmgard was quickly transformed into a Christian realm. All the Russian folk were obliged to be baptized, and only the Warangians of the Grand Prince's retinue were allowed freedom of religion. It then soon came to pass that the East Roman Emperor was badly assailed by his enemies and called on Prince Vladimir for aid. Three gold pieces for each warrior as well as the emperor's sister for his bride; that was the Prince's price. Left with little choice Basileios grudgingly accepted.
In the meantime, Grand Princess Rogeneta, who had always held her protective hand over Olaf, had been disowned by her husband. Something the young jarl and warangian chief was not pleased about.
And so six thousand warriors, many of whom were Northmen, soon marched south. Olaf Tryggvessson had remained behind in Kiev with a small company, and when the jarl in command died during the winter, the Prince of Holmgard proclaimed the young warrior jarl of all the Northmen in his realm.
Vladimir's army had successfully waged the emperor's war, and he now eagerly awaited his terms to be met. But only after threatening violence did Basileios II agree and finally sent his sister to Holmgard. Again the emperor's sister set

the condition that all the folk should be baptized. Without exception! This completely soured his mood and will to reside in Holmgard, for he was a loyal follower of the god Odin. The one eyed Father-God of the Northmen was a god of warriors and he gave the Norwegian his power and his salvation. And many Northmen soon thought the same as their jarl!

"I am weary of the service to Vladimir", Olaf said to his captains, "Perhaps this is a sign from Odin and it is time for me to go North to reclaim my inheritance".

An old captain by the name of Askold who was very fond of the young chieftain immediately agreed. "Olaf has always led us well and he is of the lineage of Harald Fairhair! So why not?"

The under-chieftains and captains of the Warangians who were present all nodded in agreement.

"He shall remain our jarl and leader", Askold spoke, "For his favor with the gods is great! Odin loves this warrior! Let him lead us from this country back to our home!"

In secret the Vikings boarded their long-boats and sailed across the Black Sea to the mouth of the Dniepr River. Only those few Northmen who had already founded families remained in the realm of Vladimir and were baptized. But when the Prince of Holmgard heard of their flight he was deeply enraged and ordered the chieftains of the wild steppe tribes to deny the deserters passage through their lands. Not all obeyed, but most did, and so many skirmishes were fought that cost the lives of many Vikings in the young jarls band. And despite losing nearly half of his men they stilled reached the shores of the Baltic Sea. Only eight long-boats, albeit fully manned, remained after reaching the borders of the land of the Poles. Heavy rains and icy winds forced the men to interrupt their journey north, and they decided to row into the next river mouth they would find. They followed a channel between two islands that led them into a backwater, which they crossed and led them further up river where they soon came upon a city. It was the city of Jomsborg[9] with its great keep, from which the widely feared Jomsvikings[10] ruled. They were subjects of the Danish King Sweyn Forkbeard and their leader a jarl named Palnatoki of Fyn. The Jomsvikings lived their lives according to strict rules and laws and this was their strength. There was not a man over fifty among them and each one had to vouch unconditionally for the other. If a Jomsviking was killed dishonorably, his comrades would avenge him. Olaf also learned that this was actually the realm of the Polish king Mieszko, who resided in his capital city of Poznan only two days ride away. But he did not dare expel the Danish Vikings from his lands.

The ships followed the broad river known as the Oder. After a day and a night they reached a fork and the left river, which the Poles called the Warta led directly to the capital city of the realm. The Vikings made camp on the shores of the Warta not far from Poznan, which was built on an island in the river. And Jarl Olaf readied his long-boat to sail to the city for he wished to request of the ruler that his Viking band may winter in the realm of the Poles.

After several merchants and other foreign visitors Olaf Tryggvesson was finally admitted to King Mieszko's presence. And when the young Jarl Olaf, who was barely nineteen years old, briefly recounted his life's story to the Polish court, all present, but particularly the ladies were touched by the tale of the young prince, who had lived his youth as a slave. This Viking was special, the king promptly

---

9 Jomsborg is used exclusively in the Nordic Sagas, while medieval German histories refer to the town as Jumne.
10 A feared band of staunchly Pagan Viking mercenaries.

realized. For a lad so young to rally an army of vicious sea warriors behind him had to be extraordinary indeed. And since Olaf was the son of a king, Mieszko invited him to stay the winter in Poznan. Such a far traveled guest – particularly one who knew so much about his powerful neighbor Vladimir – was very welcome to Mieszko indeed. Olaf sent word to his band of warriors to erect a camp down river in which they would wait out the winter safe and warm. The jarl himself remained in Poznan with a just few men as guards, and enjoyed the comforts of the court. Despite being a Christian country and the King a devout follower of the Christian God, he benevolently overlooked the Pagan inclinations of the Vikings. They were after all brave and capable warriors, the likes of which a king would gladly see at his side.

Especially the eldest son of the Polish King concerned himself with the Viking jarl, and the young men, who were of similar age, were soon bound together in a semblance of friendship. For Boleslaw did not press him with attempts at conversion as others did.

There was also a young woman at the court, and his heart had been enflamed by her since that very first day he stood before the *druzhina*[11]. Her name was Geira and she was the eldest of Mieszko's three daughters. Soon Olaf's love for her grew immeasurably and it pained him greatly that the young lady should seem so unobtainable. The love-stricken warrior even followed the royal family into the church for mass, just to catch a glimpse of Geira. And so the jarl grew ever more sorrowful and his mood ever darker. Until finally Prince Boleslaw asked what was troubling him.

"It is a woman, is it not?", the Polish prince asked laughing, and Olaf coyly looked away. "She is of high birth and you believe her to be unapproachable!"

---

[11] The Polish royal court.

Olaf nodded and Boleslaw cordially patted his shoulder. "Surely there is a way to your love, Olaf", the Prince spoke comfortingly, "I will help you, if it is in my power. But be certain of one thing – if it is a girl of the *druzhina* you will have to renounce your gods and pray to the Lord Christ henceforth!"

The men living in Poznan with Olaf also noticed the mood of their jarl.
"We are Vikings! We will simply drag her to our ship and leave Poland!", Askold suggested.
"Have you gone mad? Old fool!" Olaf was shocked for he would never have considered taking Geira by force. And so he was forced to continue to endure his anguish, with only the hope of occasionally catching a glance of the beautiful maiden.

Then it so happened that one evening Olaf entered the church. He could not explain it himself, how his path had brought him, a Viking and staunch follower of Odin, there of all places. And as he paced passed the pews he noticed a figure in the first row, clad in a precious robe with the hood covering its face. The person was deep in prayer and had not yet noticed the jarl. Slowly he approached the first pews that were reserved for the royal family. His heart started pounding rapidly. What if it was her? Hesitantly he came closer and when he saw that it was indeed Princess Geira sitting there praying, his heart leaped. She slowly lifted her head and when their eyes met a shy smile lit up her beautiful face.
Now Olaf mustered all of his courage and knelt down beside the beloved girl. "Now or never", he whispered to himself. "Though this may cause me to be led to the gallows tomorrow, I must confess my love for you, Princess Geira!"

Never in his wildest dreams had Olaf thought he would utter words such as these.

"My heart burns for you, dear Geira, and you must know it before I leave your fair country!"

"You are leaving Poland?", the Princess asked alarmed, "But why?"

"I can fight men and fear not the sharpness of their blades, but I cannot endure the pains of unrequited love any longer!"

"Oh, my Olaf. My foolish Olaf, I love you too!"

Her beautiful eyes shone like gemstones as she spoke. She leaned forward and kissed the blonde warrior intimately and had it become known, it would have indeed cost the young jarl his head.

"It's Geira!" Boleslaw cried in shock when the couple called upon the Prince for his help. "The King will never allow this marriage!"

"Surely my father has other plans for his oldest daughter", he said and his irritation was visible. "She will marry a lord or even a king. As a pledge of peace!"

"No, I will not!", Geira said stubbornly, "If I cannot marry Olaf we will both go to our deaths!"

The Prince looked at his sister with dismay. "Is your love for one another so great?", he asked, and the couple nodded. The Prince remained silent for a moment, thinking. "I will help you, like I promised. But rest assured this will not be easy".

Prince Boleslaw was a skilled and diplomatic speaker and possessed enough cunning to contend with the King's stubbornness. And so the Prince was able to wring his father's permission for the marriage with a ruse.

But King Mieszko was so angered by this coup that he set Boleslaw back in the line of succession. And Geira, too received her punishment. Since she was marrying a mere jarl, her dowry would be no greater than that of a common merchant's daughter. But the greatest punishment was to go to the Viking who dared ask the hand of a royal princess. He was to be baptized and forever swear off his gods.

But Mieszko was no fool and knew of the cunning of the Northmen. He had often heard that they allowed themselves to be sprinkled with holy water just to trade in Christian cities.

No! Olaf would become a true Christian. He would go to church every Sunday and on the first, the King ordered him to sit on the last bench in the very back. With every visit he would be allowed to move up one bench. Furthermore, he would be taught about the Christian faith by the bishop himself, and so many weeks passed. But this time passed like sand in an hourglass, and one day the court celebrated the wedding of Princess Geira with the warrior Olaf Tryggvesson.

A whole year went by and it was the happiest time in the life of Olaf the Norwegian. And though he had to maintain his position of leader of the Vikings by fighting several duels, he wielded his sword with great skill, and slowly he began to realize that the strength and favor of the Lord Christ had to be greater than that of Odin. He had built for himself a large house and farm and when Geira was soon with child his happiness was then complete.

But then it came to pass that some Polish towns were attacked by enemy tribes from north of the realm, and Prince Boleslaw saw an opportunity to rise in the esteem of his father, if only he could retake them. He asked for Olaf's aid and he was only to happy to help his brother-in-law. And so a Polish army marched by land and a Viking fleet sailed by water northwards.

After many hard battles the Polish Prince and the Viking jarl had driven the invaders away. The towns were freed and the leaders of the tribes swore to keep the peace. But when the Vikings saw the rooftops and towers of Poznan after their long journey home, they gasped in shock.

Black clouds of smoke filled the sky and a great host was besieging the gates. Olaf instantly knew who was stretching his hand out to take Poznan.

Jarl Palnatoki, the old leader of the Jomsvikings, had been called to his gods and Jarl Sigvaldi, his successor, had in his greed tripled the *danegeld*[12] of the Poles.

King Mieszko could not afford this sum, however, and so the Jomsvikings attacked Poznan to take it. Olaf knew his small band would be of little use here, particularly since Boleslaw's army was still on the march. And so he decided to sail for Jomsborg.

With a ruse they were able to gain entry into the well defended keep and afterwards, defeating the few remaining warriors was easy, for it was only a small guard with sick and wounded among them. A courier brought Jarl Sigvaldi the message that the Jomsburg was in the hands of Olaf Tryggvesson and so he was forced to lift his siege of Poznan. Jarl Sigvaldi was forced to submit to the Polish King and swear an oath of fealty to Mieszko otherwise the infamous Jomsburg would have gone up in flames.

Olaf Tryggvesson was celebrated as the hero and liberator of the Polish realm, but fate had dealt him a harsh blow. His beloved Geira had died in childbirth, for her weakened body could not survive the strains of the siege. Great sadness was felt throughout Poland and the people grieved with Viking jarl.

---

12 Tribute, protection money against Viking raids.

But no comfort or succor could help Olaf overcome the grief of his loss. More and more he took his leave of the court and spent his time with his warriors in their great encampment on the banks of the river. Filled with anger and rage and more often than not drunk, he cursed the Lord Christ, who had taken the dearest thing on earth away from him, and he proclaimed he would make sacrifices to Odin once again. This angered the bishop of Poznan so greatly that he demanded the King drive the Viking out of the country. But Olaf Tryggvesson had lost all joy of living in Poland and after the winter – it was the year 991 AD – he left the realm of King Mieszko to go raiding.

*

Three long years had passed during which Olaf Tryggvesson afflicted the coasts of the North Sea as a feared Viking and sea-king. For over two years alone he laid waste to the coasts of Scotland, pillaging and plundering what he could from the villages and towns. At the best of times his fleet was over thirty ships strong, and many a king would ask for the fealty of the young sea-king.
And Olaf was once again firm in his faith in Odin and Thor and Freyja and all the other gods who dwelled in Asgard[13]. He fully believed again that it was they, who ruled his fortunes.

In the spring of 993 AD the fleet of Olaf Tryggvesson had shrunk considerably. Many captains had grown tired of taking orders from someone else, and had made off to try their luck alone. During this summer, the Isle of Iona was to suffer bitterly at the hands of the savage sea-warriors, as it

---

13 Asgard and Midgard: The realm of the gods and the realm of men.

so often had in the past. And many towns in Wales were pillaged. Then the Vikings raided Ireland.
They seized many merchant vessels, and also a nunnery fell victim to the Vikings. The Brides of Christ suffered greatly and many were reminded of the attack months later, when they gave birth to a child. In the fall, the ships of Olaf sailed through a great storm and many were scattered in all directions. Olaf himself barely reached Normandy with only a handful of *snekkjas*. Here he bid the Norman duke of Rouen to winter in his lands and the duke happily agreed. He always received Northern visitors gladly, for his roots were in Norway.

In the spring of 994, however, the Viking jarl set sail once again with fifteen ships to go a viking[14]. He graciously declined the duke's offer to stay with his court. Slowly the number of ships grew, for many ship owners were prepared to follow the famous sea-king and expected great wealth from swearing him fealty.
And so the warriors came to the shores of Britain, and Olaf joined the ranks of the Danish king Sweyn Forkbeard, who was laying siege to the capital of London with a great fleet. Olaf hoped to acquire enough wealth to return to Norway and claim his inheritance. But the news the Viking jarl then heard confused him greatly.
In the realm of the Poles, Boleslav had succeeded his father Mieszko upon his death, which pleased Olaf greatly. And King Sweyn of Denmark was now Boleslav's brother-in-law, for he had wed his sister Gunhild some time ago. Thus the danger of a Danish invasion of Poland was dispelled, for the kingdoms had long been in argument over the lands of Pomerania. And even Jarl Sigvaldi, the leader of the Jomsvikings, was now an in-law of the Polish king. He had

---

[14] Pirate Cruise

arranged the alliance between Boleslav and the Dane, and had been rewarded with the hand of the beautiful Astrid, youngest sister of the king.

Including Olaf's thirty two ships, over three hundred warships now lay at the shores of the Thames.
Nearly five thousand warriors assaulted the walls of the city. Sweyn Forkbeard had London in his iron grasp, but he could not breach the sturdy fortifications, which were brimming with Britannic warriors. Furthermore, the Anlgo-Saxon king Aethelred was not in London. He had withdrawn to th safety of Winchester, and was sending a host to free London from the clutches of the Northmen. But the Vikings soundly defeated these reinforcements, and Aethelred offered the Northmen a ransom.
Sixteen thousand pounds of silver were demanded by Sweyn! And in order to save his capital, the king of the Britons reluctantly paid the sum.
But when the time came to divide the spoils, the king of the Danes and Olaf Tryggvesson got into a great argument. For Olaf, who was a free sea-king and should have received a substantial portion, received no more than a common steersman. But despite his anger he could do nothing.
The following night Olaf and his men secretly rowed down the Thames and out into the open sea. Only half of his men and fourteen ships remained. His dream of returning to Norway seemed farther away than ever.

It was already late in the summer when the Vikings arrived on one of the Scilly Islands and made camp. Here they planned to heal their wounds and decide on what to do the rest of the summer. There was a monastery located on a steep cliff not far from their camp, and some of the men thought it best to plunder the temple of the Christians, but

Olaf rejected the suggestion and the warriors muttered in discontent. Things were not looking good for the young sea-king. Their spoils were to few! Too few for all of the captains, and many thought that Odin's blessing had left the jarl. And so it happened that one of the captains, who had long envied Olaf's leadership, sneaked into his tent during the night and rammed his sword into Olaf's chest while he slept.

When the morning came, Olaf was heavily wounded and most of his men had left with the mutineer. They had stolen all of the treasure and had sailed out to sea. Only a handful of loyal men remained, barely two crews.

But Olaf was grievously injured and it was doubtful he would live to see the next day. And so one of the men who had been with him since Holmgard took his courage together and brought the wounded Olaf to the abbey on the cliffs. He knew of the leechcraft of the Christian priests and they began their work without question. They made a bed for Olaf and cared for him day and night. But it still took a month for the mortally wounded to recover.

"The Lord Jesus Christ has worked a miracle on you", the abbot spoke softly, as Olaf finally opened his eyes. "Surely you have great deeds to yet accomplish, my son!"

"I wish to pray", the convalescent said weakly, and the surprised abbot prayed the Lord's Prayer with the Northman. On this day, Olaf had found his way back to the Christian God. And when his men heard about his recovery, they too desired to be baptized, for they had never witnessed a man recover from such an injury before.

The god of these friars must be a mighty god indeed. And after a while Olaf left the Scilly Islands with his two ships and returned to the kingdom of Aethelred. But this time it was not to plunder and pillage. Carrying a message from the

abbot, Olaf traveled to Winchester to seek out Archbishop Aelfheah.
Seeing the man who had harried the coasts of Britain for four summers standing before him with a letter from an abbot astonished him greatly. But the desire of the former sea-king to return to the communion of Christians surprised and pleased the bishop. He sent the former enemy of Britain with a letter to the court of King Aethelred in London. Aethelred, too, was greatly surprised to see Olaf standing before him as a converted and penitent sinner. And Aethelred would have been a poor king, had he not known how to use this to his advantage. He proclaimed that the Christian religion would prohibit the Vikings from raiding and murdering and so the solution should be to convert Northmen to the true faith. The feared Olaf Tryggvesson, offspring of Harald Fairhair, was living proof of his words.

A few days later Olaf was baptized a second time in the cathedral of London. It was on a Sunday when Bishop Aelfeah sprinkled the holy water on the feared Viking's brow and King Aethelred himself was Olaf's godfather. The king let news of the Viking jarl's conversion be known in all of his realm.
Aethelred II, whom his people disparagingly called "the Unready", for he had been unable to stop the Vikings from invading, knew only too well, how quickly Northmen could change their minds. Olaf was living proof of this, for he had already been baptized in Poland and abandoned the true faith.
"Hear me, Olaf Tryggvesson", the king spoke after summoning the jarl to his halls, "Not too long ago, one of my Earls died in Wales. He left behind a young widow called Lady Gydia. She would be a bride befitting of your rank!"

Olaf stared at him in amazement for he currently had no interest in marriage. "You honor me with your offer, King Aethelred. But I had not thought to take another wife".
"Don't be hasty, Olaf", the Briton sternly replied, "Lady Gydia is a beautiful woman! She is Irish by birth yet in her veins flows Nordic blood. And I can tell you, her lands are vast. You would profit greatly from it and in a few years, you could raise a mighty army!"
The king paused a moment to let his words sink in. "Was it not your intention to some day return to Norway to claim your inheritance?"
And that very day the king sent a herald to Lady Gydia with the marriage proposal. And soon afterward, Olaf Tryggvesson traveled to Wales himself to negotiate the wedding with the young widow, and he was received warmly.

The ceremony between Olaf Tryggvesson and Lady Gydia was held after the Christian fashion, for the fair woman was quickly taken by the appearance of the blonde Norwegian. He had proven himself the rightful husband for the Irishwoman in a duel with a rival, and the lady soon agreed to the marriage. In late autumn the couple sailed to Ireland, where Gydia's family had great influence. She introduced the Norwegian as her new husband, and here too, he was greeted warmly, as he was of the house of Harald Finehair, just as here family.

They wished to stay the winter of the year 994 on to 995 in Dublin and before the first snow had fallen, a Norse merchant ship arrived in the harbor.
Onboard the knarr[15] was a man named Thorir Klakka. This man had embarked on a long voyage, for the knarr came

---

15 Knarr: fat-bellied Norse merchant vessel.

from Trøndelag, an area in northwestern Norway, and had sailed by London to Wales. But Thorir Klakka did not find what he sought there, and so his voyage took him to Ireland, where he finally found his goal. Finally he stood before the man who was the cause for his long journey. The feared and famous sea-king, Olaf Tryggvesson! Olaf was very pleased by the visit of his countryman and eagerly listened to what he had to say.

"Are you Olaf Tryggvesson, of whom all Thule speaks?", he inquired cautiously. "The sea-king and Viking jarl? The son of King Tryggve of Ranrike?"

Olaf nodded and stared at the stranger in surprise, who smiled as if relieved of a great burden.

"It is no coincidence that I stand here before you, Jarl Olaf", he began to report, "The folk of Trøndelag suffer greatly under the lordship of Jarl Hakon of Lade. He has proclaimed himself their king and violates the law everyday as he pleases. He and his retinue go from homestead to homestead, eating the farmers' storehouses empty and no young girl nor married woman is safe from the jarl's lust!"

Olaf raised an eyebrow, but remained silent and continued to listen.

"Now the folky of Trøndelag send me to you, Olaf Tryggvesson, to offer you the crown! Come with your mighty fleet and free us from the evil jarl!"

"I must disappoint you, Thorir Klakka", Olaf spoke calmly, "It is true, once I had a great fleet and many warriors to man it. But now I have only two ships and no more than a hundred men, who follow the Lord Jesus Christ, as I do!"

The messenger was surprised and visibly disapointed.

"The folk of Trøndelag believe firmly in the old Gods and will not have a Christian king on the throne", he said grimly.

"Should I ever become king, I would make the Christian faith law", Olaf said honestly, and Thorir was unhappy with this. Should his long, arduous voyage have been for nought? "Remember that the men of Trøndelag are renowned for their stubbornness. Don't force them to abandon the old Gods", the messenger spoke calmly, "Otherwise you'll end up like Hakon!"

Olaf Tryggvesson invited the emissary from Trøndelag to winter in his halls. And so they had plenty of time to discuss the matter. But it soon became apparent that Lady Gydia had no wish to leave her home and follow Olaf to Norway. Thorir Klakka fearing for his mission had one final card to play. Slowly spring followed winter and the jarl had even managed to convince Thorir to get baptized. Yet Olaf still had no wish to leave his beloved wife to become king of a people who would despise him. Now the messenger saw the time come, to tell Olaf what he really knew. The fire was crackling in the great hearth of the guest hall where the jarl and several of his Irish family and Thorir Klakka were sitting. Presently the Trøndner began to tell a story which he had heard in Sotenäset.

Olaf pricked his ears at the sound of the name of that city which had been the royal city of Ranrike. It was the saga of the Flight of Queen Astrid that Thori was recounting.

"But that is my mother!", the jarl called out astonished, "Speak, Thorri! Tell me what you know and I will repay you every word in gold!"

"Oh, I have no need of a reward, but I will tell you what I have heard", the Trøndner said humbly. "Astrid, the woman who in first marriage was wife to King Tryggve returned to Norway as a slave."

"First marriage ... and she returned to Norway, you say? Does that mean my mother yet lives?", Olaf asked excitedly.

"Well, I cannot say for certain, but they say that the former queen was bought and freed by a farmer from Offrigstad. Out of gratitude she agreed to become his wife and gave him three more children, so they say. It has been a long time since I heard this tale, so I cannot claim to know if the wife of Tryggve of Ranrike, the former Queen Astrid is still among the living."

"I must travel to Norway immediately. Time is short!"

In the following days the jarl made preparations to sail to Norway, the home he left as an infant. And even though his wife Gydia bade him remain in Wales, he soon assembled warriors who were to sail with him. Since Olaf only wanted baptized men at his side, he was only able to man five longships. But these men swore him an oath of loyalty far different to the pagan one. They forfeited their right to co-determination, as was common with Vikings, and swore him absolute loyalty.

"I will not due battle with Hakon, should the words of Thorir Klakka turn out to be false", the jarl said to his wife on the day of the departure, "then I will seek out my relatives and look for my mother. I will return to you by autumn."

Sadly Gydia gave her blessing to Olaf's voyage. What else could she do? It was already decided!

The longships of Olaf Tryggvesson were still on the North Sea when rebellion broke out against the petty-king of Trøndelag. Jarl Hakon's desire of the wife of a wealthy farmer had been the final straw. In great anger, the jarls sent the arrow of war through the land, summoning a great peasant army to face the evil jarl.

Jarl Hakon took refuge in the mountains with his retinue and his son Erlend, who lived in the city of Lade in the great Fjord of Trondheim, was given the order to take the three long ships of Hakon to Møre. But at just that moment the five ships of Olaf reached the fjord and when he saw the banner the ships were flying he ordered his men to attack.

The ships of the wicked Jarl Hakon were quickly boarded and Erlend fell dying into the black depths.

Now the great-grandson of Harald Fairhair was welcomed in Lade as a liberator and celebrated by the folk of the Trøndner. And soon thereafter the chieftains and free peasants called for a *thing* to choose a new leader.

Thorir Klakka suggested the son of Tryggve should be king, for he was of the house of Harald Fairhair. And many agreed! But there was still the issue of religion. But when Olaf agreed to respect the old faith the most influential chieftains and headmen voted for the great-grandson of the great King Harald.

In the summer of 995 AD, Olaf Tryggvesson was proclaimed king of the realm of Jarl Hakon.

*

After the new king Olaf had sailed south with a vast fleet and had either killed or driven off all the supporters and friends of the old king Hakon, he was able to unite the districts of western Norway under his rule.

It was already late summer when Olaf Tryggvesson began retaking southern Norway which had been occupied by the Danes. One Danish jarl after the other had to concede defeat before the new king of the Norwegians. And not all of them accepted the generous offer of safe passage. King Sweyn Forkbeard was none too pleased at the loss of the southern Norwegian districts, for he pressed a great deal of taxes out of the people there. And yet, a swift reconquest was not in sight for he had set his gaze upon the island of the Angles and Saxons, which he ravished from the Danelaw[16].

---

16 Danelaw: Area in eastern England which was occupied and settled by the Danes.

Unlike in the western districts, the new king only installed Christian jarls in the districts of Viken[17]. Now finally, after even the head of the wicked Jarl Hakon was thrown at his feet, could Olaf Tryggvesson finally start looking for his family.

And soon his search was at an end. Just as Thorir Klakka had said, the former Queen Astrid was living in the hinterlands of Offrigstad as a simple peasant's wife. And with great joy Olaf saw that his mother, his elder sisters and his three half-siblings were all well. Though the hair of the former queen was showing signs of grey she was still in good health and had even come into a small fortune.

Before the onset of winter, his relatives moved into the royal hall of Sotenäset at Olaf's wish. Olaf Tryggvesson had united all the districts and ruled as king over all of Norway.

But in the spring of 996, Olaf began his Christian conversion work. First the people of Sotenäset had to be baptized, for the king did not wish to live with pagans in his city. Then the king sent out his warriors and in all of southern Norway up to the river Gøtelielva, the border river between his realm and Sweyn's, he destroyed all the pagan temples and burned the idols.

All folk were forced at swordpoint to be baptized. But by autumn Olaf felt the repercussions of his zealotry. The jarls of northern and western Norway were angered by Olaf's forced conversions and accused him of breaking his word and refused to pay taxes. The tax collectors and royal officials were quickly thrown out.

And so in the following spring the king sailed forth with an army to Trøndelag to force the jarls back under his control. But the jarls of Agder, Møre and Lade had assembled a large army to confront the king.

---

17 Viken: Historical name for the southern districts of Norway.

When Olaf saw this he sent messengers to the jarls to offer negotiations. Most of the chieftains rejoiced at this for they thought they had beaten the king. And at their *thing* they demanded Olaf participate in their pagan rituals.
"You demand that I, a devout Christian, make a bloody sacrifice to your devilish idols?", the king shouted angrily into the hall, "But I will do as you ask!"
Now the jarls were certain they had brought the King of Norway to his knees, but they were mistaken. "But since I am a king and not a common peasant", Olaf spoke calmly, "you cannot ask that I sacrifice common slaves upon the stone altar. Only those of high birth shall die by my knife!"
The king spoke the names of several jarls from Trøndelag. Immediately armed men stormed into the hall and arrested the ones named. The shock among the other jarls, chieftains and freemen was great, but they could do nothing at blade point.

In the following days the relatives of the prisoners came forth an begged for mercy for the heads of their families. They promised to be baptized and honor the Lord Jesus Christ. And this included of course the folk in their households and retinues. The king agreed to this and the jarls of Trondheimfjord all knelt before the Christian priests and were daubed with holy water. Many peasants followed their example, and when one gothi[18] spoke out angrily against the king he was killed by the people without hesitation.
Now Olaf Tryggvesson was in good hope that the jarls of Trøndelag would stay true to their oaths. But no sooner had he returned to the royal city of Sotenäset, was he already hearing disconcerting news about rebellious gothar who

---

18 Gothi, pl. gothar: Chieftain with the function of a priest in Germanic Paganism.

were rousing the northern folk against him. But the jarls kept their word, in part because Olaf had taken their firstborn children as hostages. Their fear for their offspring was too great to rebel. The hostages themselves however were treated well by Olaf. They received a Christian education so that the girls could serve at court and the boys could serve in the king's army. But the gothar of Trøndelag for the most part ended up burned at the stake.

*

In the year 998 AD Olaf had built a large royal palace on the fjord at the banks of the Nid river. He wished to avoid another rebellion by the jarls of West Norway. Soon a large city sprung up around it called Nidaros. In the same year Olaf, implored by his councilors, entered into marriage negotiations. Sigrid Storrada, the dowager queen of Sweden would be the chosen bride.
Sigrid, whom some called "the Haughty" ruled at the side of her son, who was still quite young and called the "lap king". All of Thule said that she was a beautiful woman but of bad character. Moreover she was a priestess of Freyr and gladly gave herself over to men during fertility rituals. Sigrid believed firmly in the old gods and this would soon become a problem.

Winter had fallen and the snows lay high in the borderlands between Norway and Sweden when the king rode out in his sleigh to the city of Kungälv where the negotiations were to take place. And finally after days of waiting the Queen of Sweden arrived at the arranged meeting place. But the regent let the highborn suitor wait for two days more until she accepted his invitation. King Olaf however was much impressed by the woman for she was slender in build, had long blonde hair and a very beautiful face. But soon the charming Sigrid showed her true face, for the negotiations did not go as the councilors of the highnesses had hoped. Sigrid demanded more and more and soon her conditions became ever more brazen.

King Olaf however made concessions, because for him all that matter was arranging an alliance against the power hungry king of Denmark. But then she came to the point that was most important to the Norwegian: the belief in the Christian God!

King Olaf was not willing to have a pagan at his side. And so he demanded Sigrid be baptized, even in pretense. At this the beautiful queen flew into a rage. "Never will I pay homage to a slave god!", she cried out angrily, "Freyr will take his favor from me and my womb will become barren!" Insults of the worst kind were hurled at the king and as Olaf had partaken heavily of mead that night misfortune soon struck. "You miserable whore of Freyr dare insult me! Never will I suffer a Swedish bitch by my side!", he yelled drunkenly and angrily and gave the queen a hefty slap. Instantly the warriors drew their swords and the councilors had their hands full with preventing a bloodbath. The next morning the Swedish Queen left the border town of Kungälf swearing revenge and Olaf knew he mad made a new and dangerous enemy.

In early spring of the year 999 AD messengers came to the court of Nidaros reporting the King Sweyn of Denmark had banished his wife Gunnhild to the Danelaw. And by summer there was tell in Thule that Sweyn had chosen a new consort. It was the Swedish queen Sigrid the Haughty. This was bad news for the realm of Norway for it was obvious that this marriage was a military alliance against King Olaf Tryggvesson. Sigrid was making good on the threats she had made against King Olaf. Besides the loss of southern Norway there was another thorn in the side of the Danish king. That was the lack of rulership over the Jomsvikings. Since the Odervikings were bound by oath to the Polish king Boleslav who was a friend of the Norwegian, there was a chance that he could send them to the aid of his former in-law. And even the Danish king feared the might of the warriors of Jomsburg.

Now the King Sweyn had a younger sister named Thyri. She was fair and like her father Harald before her she was of the Christian faith. She even had a monk as a foster father. But it was thanks to the spitefulness of Sigrid that Sweyn sent a messenger to the land of the Poles to offer Thyri's hand in marriage to Boleslav. The wife of the Polish king had died and he was not averse to the notion. A marriage union with the Danes reduced the probability of war after all. King Sweyn and his wife Sigrid spoke at length with Princess Thyri, but Thyri Haraldsdottir refused to wed the Polish king. To great was her fear that she would be treated as harshly as the Polish princess Gunnhild was treated at the side of her brother Sweyn. But Sigrid's spitefulness showed itself again; where first she tried coaxing her gently, her words now became harsh and wrathful. And when she threatened to feed the Christian monk who had become Thyri's friend to wild dogs, the princess complied fearful and humiliated. But only on the condition that she receive the royal treasure as a dowry.
Sweyn unhappily agreed for his coffers were dangerously empty after the wars in Britain.
King Sweyn of Denmark entrusted the jarl of Jomsburg with tying the knot with Poland. For despite Sigvaldi's oath to Boleslav he was still a faithful subject of his.

It was summer when the fleet of Sweyn Forkbeard arrived at the Jomsburg to begin the marriage negotiations. The Dane had no wish to travel to Poznan for he deemed the risk too great. Sweyn was not well liked in Poland for his occupation of Pommerania. The Danes were greeted warmly at the Jomsburg however. As a guest of Jarl Sigvaldi the king was safe!
The negotiations with Boleslav didn't take long and after half a month the Danish fleet sailed north again. Princess Thyri who was now Queen of Poland remained at the side of Bolelsav. But the young queen felt very uncomfortable in Poland and refused herself to her husband who was many years her elder. She stilled feared to be treated as poorly as his sister had in Denmark. Only the priest who loyally stayed by her side did she trust entirely, and soon she ordered him to prepare their escape from Poland.
Norway would be their destination!

It was autumn when Princess Thyri arrived at the royal court of Nidaros and fell upon her knees in front of King Olaf. The Norwegian King's palace seemed to her the only safe place from the reprisals of Sweyn Forkbeard. Both Kings hated each other. Furthermore, Olaf was known to be a good Christian and so the princess hoped to find refuge at his court. And so it was.

Thyri told the entire story of her marriage to Boleslav and King Olaf quickly saw through Sweyn's and Sigrid's fiendish plot. On Olaf's command the bishop of Nidaros annulled the mariage, for it had been forced upon Thyri by pagans. And so in the eyes of the Church Princess Thyri was a free woman once more. And now it came to pass that Olaf took a liking to the Danish princess and she was not averse

to him either. Winter came soon and before Christmas a wedding was celebrated in Nidaros.
When Sweyn heard about his sister's flight from Poland he and Sigrid were livid with rage. Now that he had heard of her marriage to King Olaf he disowned her and threatened any man who would aid her with death.

The winter of 999 AD was cold, long and dark. All commerce had come to a halt, as had the raids and wars of the Vikings. The time was passed with large feasts and the court of Norway was no exception.
Often the young queen lamented the loss of her family treasure which she had left behind during her escape from Poland. And just as often she had asked her husband to retrieve it for her. For despite all that had happened, Olaf and Boleslav bore each other no ill will.
"It is currently far to dangerous for me to leave my country, beloved Thyri", Olaf often put her off.

But at a great feast Thyri stood up and asked Olaf again to bring her treasure to Norway. And yet again Olaf refused and his councilors breathed sighs of relief.
But now Thyri acted defiantly and unreasonably like a stubborn child. "Is my husband, the King of the Norwegians, not man enough to take on his enemies for his wife?", Thyri shouted angrily across the hall and the court fell silent. Blinded by greed for gold and silver she ranted and none of the councilors could dissuade her.
"Are you a coward, who's courage shrinks at the thought of the great Sweyn Forkbeard?"
Olaf Tryggvesson stood up from his high seat, and his slight staggering showed that he had drunk plenty of mead. This humiliation could have dire consequences for Thyri but despite all expectations the king remained calm.

"If my wife values her family treasure so much she would call me a coward in front of my entire court, then I will fulfill her wish! Come summer I will equip a fleet and sail to Poland!"

The words were spoken and so there was no turning back for King Olaf Tryggvesson, if he didn't want to lose face. And though later the young queen regretted her words and bade him not make the journey, the king's decision was made.

*

As he had promised, in the year 1000 AD the king assembled a great fleet of ships at Nidaros. The jarls of all districts had to supply ships and men for Olaf Tryggvesson. Very soon over sixty longships were assembled before the city and the greatest and proudest was tied firmly to the pier of the harbor of Nidaros. It was the new ship of King Olaf. Favorable winds blew from the north when the fleet of the Norwegians set sail, and it before long they had reached the southernmost edge of the realm.

Past Lindesnes they sailed southeast and soon they reached Danish waters. Along the enemy coast they sailed into the great sound to pillage several small Danish islands. Sweyn Forkbeard should see that the Norwegians had no fear of him. Particularly brutal was their attack on Zealand where they barbarically killed, pillaged and raped the coastal villages.
After three days they had reached the narrow channel between the islands of Wolin and Usedom which led into the great Oder lagoon. They crossed the lagoon and sailed

into the mouth of the Oder where they soon arrived at the Jomsburg.

Here King Olaf was greeted warmly by Jarl Sigvaldi and his wife, the Polish princess Astrid. A messenger was sent to Poznan immediately to inform King Boleslav of the arrival of his former brother-in-law. With great joy he proclaimed that Olaf was welcome and that he did not at all begrudge him the marriage to Princess Thyrri. He laid the blame solely with King Sweyn, who had forced his sister into the unfortunate union. And so King Olaf travelled to Poznan, to the court of King Boleslav, after having stayed at the Jomsburg for two days as Jarl Sigvaldi's guest.

The Norwegian king spent his days happily in the royal city of the Poles, that place that had blessed him with the happiest days of his life. He visited and prayed at the grave of his beloved Geira and spent as much time as he could with his brother-in-law Boleslav. But soon troubling news reached the court. Scout ships of the Danes or Swedes had been spotted in the lagoon and this meant danger.

But it was Jarl Sigvaldi who suggested that a fleet of Jomsvikings could provide escort for the ships of King Olaf until they reached the Baltic Sea. Boleslav agreed immediately and as Olaf did not want to offend him, he accepted the offer.

The day of their departure arrived and the ships of the Norwegian King sailed back to the Jomsburg to meet with the other ships of the great fleet and to prepare for the voyage home. On a bright and warm summer's day the fleet rowed down the Oder. At the very front was the flagship, the great dragon ship of the king, followed by the fleet of the Norwegians.

The Jomsvikings of Jarl Sigvaldi were in the rear. But soon scouts further ahead reported the presence of a great war fleet that had assembled in the lagoon. And only now did Olaf see the ships of the Jomsvikings falling back and blocking the entrance of the Oder. There was now no possibility of escape!

"Sigvaldi, you miserable coward!", Olaf roared in anger, shaking his clenched fist in the air.

"I think it's worse than that", one of the king's captains said, "Sigvaldi is a traitor and in league with the Danes! It's a damned trapp!"

A ship rowed up to them with a white flag flying from the mast. The snekja came along broadside to the royal ship and Olaf Tryggvesson stepped up toward the railing.

"I am Jarl Erik, son of Jarl Hakon of Lade", the captain of the enemy ship shouted.

"I am Olaf Tryggvesson, King of Norway! Say your piece, Jarl Erik", the king responded gravely.

"I come to bring you the terms of the Kings of Denmark and Sweden!"

"You offer me terms?", Olaf laughed bitterly and threateningly, "And a Norwegian is their errand boy. We will smash your heathen skulls bloody!"

But Hakonson was not impressed. "King Sweyn will allow you free passage on the condition you swear never to return to Norway, Olaf Tryggvesson", he spoke with a sneer. "If you refuse, this will be your last day in Midgard. Decide now, shammer king!"

"The Lord Jesus Christ is on our side and he will crush you pagan scum, Jarl Erik!" Olaf Tryggvesson was convinced, the Christian God would give them power to do so.

"We will not go even one oar stroke back, tell that to King Sweyn!"

Hakonson looked at Olaf with a pleased expression on his face. "I had almost feared that that Dane would cheat me of my revenge. But today I will avenge the death of my father Hakon, Olaf!"

The ship of the fugitive Norwegian Erik Hakonson cast off and rowed back into the lagoon. Olaf quickly started giving orders, so his warriors could prepare for the imminent battle. Groups of four ships were tied together to form platforms on which the warriors could fight. Stroke for stroke they rowed out of the mouth of the Oder into the great lagoon.
And their they were met by great fleet made up of Danes, Swedes and the pagan Norwegians who had fled Olaf's conversion frenzy.
The battle was joined and no side could gain a clear advantage. Ships were captured and lost again. The blood of the warriors ran in deep red rivers across the planks of the ships and one after the other the dead fell overboard and sank beneath the dark waters.
The Norwegians fought bravely, for they knew the Lord Christ was on their side. But the greater numbers of the enemy threatened to overwhelm them, and soon the defenders were exhausted while the attackers sent fresh men against them.
And then night had fallen and brought a lull in the fighting until it stopped altogether. Now the warriors had a chance to tend to their wounds and rest. Suddenly the captains went to their king, for they thought the battle lost.
"What will happen when the sun rises?", one of Olaf's closest men asked. Olaf sighed and gave voice to what all were thinking. "I believe that I have lost the rule over Norway. But tomorrow I will die an honorable death, as is worthy of a king!"

But the captains protested, for they did not wish to see their king die. "Lord Christ preserve us", one captain said, who had fought alongside Olaf Tryggvesson since Kiev.
He looked at the others and said with a cheeky grin "A good swimmer could make it to the shores of the Polish realm. Give me your golden helm and take mine instead, King Olaf!"

It was before sunrise when the King of Norway ordered another attempt to break through the ring of enemies around them. Again fierce fighting erupted during which many men fell overboard. Amongst them was also a man who bore a golden helm. The enemy loosed their arrows at the warrior in the cold waters and stabbed at him with their spears. Shrill screams of death echoed across the water and many a man sank into the deep. But as the news was passed from ship to ship that the King of Norway had found a watery grave, the battle of the Oder lagoon ended.
Sweyn Forkbeard proclaimed generously that he would allow the surviving warriors free and honorable passage.

When the Polish king heard of Jarl Sigvaldi's treachery he was livid with anger. He had his vassal brought to Poznan and held court over him. The jarl of Jomsburg begged to be allowed to die honorably like a warrior, sword in hand, and King Boleslav realised that he still firmly believed in the old gods of the North. This enraged the king even further and he sentenced the jarl to be locked up in the dungeon for the rest of his days on water and bread and with daily floggings. This was the worst punishment imaginable to a jarl, a warrior and a feared Viking.

Some time later a priest came before the king and swore to him he had met the former king of Norway in a small chapel. The cleric swore to have known Tryggvesson's face and the man before him, dressed in the garb of a monk, had undoubtedly been King Olaf Tryggvesson.

*

4. Thangbrand the Missionary

In the early summer of the year 997 AD a Knarr, a fat-bellied ship used by the Northmen for trade, sailed from Norway to Iceland by way of the Orkney and Shetland Isles. Aboard this Knarr was a man named Thangbrand, a German religious priest who had been sent in the name of emperor Otto III as a missionary to Norway. And Thangbrand was an eager proselytizer who knew how to assert himself among the free folk who were stubborn, pigheaded and very loyal to Odin. Strong in stature and eloquent in expression, his hands would not only administer blessings, but sometimes hard knocks as well.

After some time the king of Norway heard tell of this German priest traveling his land and tirelessly preaching the love and mercy of the Lord Jesus Christ. So he had the foreigner brought to him at Nidaras, the new seat of the king. Not too long ago, the king had his new city built near Trondheimfjord at the banks of the river Nid in order to more easily control the unruly people of Trøndelag. And here too, should the priest work successfully in the name of God, for the stubborn people still made sacrifices to Odin, Freya and Thor. The king quickly took a liking to the gruff giant who would freely speak his mind even before the king. "Only the Lord Jesus Christ can order me", Thangbrand had said in his stubbornness, and the king was deeply impressed. And so it came to pass that Olaf Tryggvesson who was not only King of the Norwegians, but also a devout Christian since his youth, took the priest into his service.

To spread the true Faith he sent the man of God to the island of ice, for the Norwegian kings laid claim to Iceland, as the

forefathers of the Icelandic people came from Norway for the most part. But the Icelanders refused to acknowledge the king and they in turn had not yet dared to assert their claim with force of arms. Without hesitation the priest followed the king's order and embarked on the arduous journey, for he was no less zealous than the King of the Norwegians himself. He had forced his people with sword and axe to abandon the old Northern gods and pray to the Lord Christ. And since his army was strong and he also used the taxes placed on Norwegian goods as leverage, the jarls and chieftains were all to often forced to bow to the will of Tryggvesson.
And so this Thangbrand came to Iceland as a missionary. The people of Reykjavik greeted him warmly. Most Icelanders prayed to the Aesir, but there were already some Christian farmers on the island. Yet faith in the old gods predominated. But since religious freedom was practiced in Iceland, most people did not care to which god their neighbors prayed. And the *gothi* too, tolerated those of different faith, so long as they kept quiet.

Thangbrand immediately went to work and preached the Word of God, as ordered by the king. And so he managed to win some undecided people, mostly common folk and slaves, for the Lord Jesus Christ. But the ears of the people of position and power, the jarls and wealthy farmers, remained deaf to the priest's words. And slowly the mood soured toward the Norwegian King's missionary.
Partly because his preaching was becoming increasingly brash and demanding. The hot-tempered man treated the people of Reykjavik with mounting condescension day by day, and he made no attempts to hide the fact that he despised the followers of the Aesir.

Many a Christian farmer warned the stout priest of the *gothi*, but the man of God would not be dissuaded. His brashness reached its peak at the *thing*. He demanded the jarls build a church and demolish the pagan temples.
The outrage was great, but not enough, Thangbrand cursed the *gothi*, blasphemed Odin and Thor, named Freya a whore and threatened to call upon the armies of the King of Norway, should his demands be unfulfilled.

Several days after the assembly, two men of the *gothi* of Reykjavik rode to the cottage of Thangbrand and his followers. They were to persuade the priest to leave, for his presence in Iceland was no longer wished. But the missionary bluntly refused to leave the smoky and stormy bay of Reykjavik. And so the men began to quarrel. Fierce insults were traded, and the Icelanders, threatening violence demanded the priest finally leave their island. "No one will dare drive me from this island!", Thangbrand cried out. Quickly he picked up a pitch fork leaning against a wall and angrily rammed it into his adversary's chest. At once the second Icelander drew his sword, but at that moment the pitch fork's shaft cracked him on the head, causing him to stumble back. Livid with rage the priest threw down the farming tool and picked up the blade of the slain man at his feet. He swung with all of his might at the Icelander's head, until he too sank dying to his knees. When his companions had seen what the militant priest had done, they hastily buried the dead and suggested they leave. That same night the warlike cleric Thangbrand fled Reykjavik.

Again he sailed along the coast, this time back east, and he went ashore in Reydarfjord. But to his great delight the folk there had already been baptized, so there was no work for him there. After a few day he left the fjord and sailed northwards up the eastern coast.

After the knarr had passed the island of Grimsey it turned into the great Eyjarfjord, and Thangbrand went ashore at the town of Ravnswik. Here too, he received friendly welcome for the news of his manslaughter had not yet reached the north of the island. He and his companions moved into a longhouse offered to them by the townsfolk on the edge of the settlement. A portion of the people of Ravnswik had already been baptized as well, and they were happy to see a priest. Mostly they were wealthy merchants and their kin who did trade in the lands of the German Emperor and there had taken on the new faith. Many hoped the monk would stay forever and helped him any way they could. And Thangbrand's work quickly bore fruit. He preached and the people came to be baptized. He could even move the *thing* to erect a church, and he started construction that same summer.

But the wealthy farmers of the area, who were all followers of Odin met in secret. At this *thing* did they hope to decide on how to proceed with the intrusive priest, and they quickly agreed to have him done away with. A servant who was promised land in exchange for carrying out the murder was eager to kill the shammer[19].

One evening a man rode up to the house of Thangbrand. He implored the priest to follow him quickly, for a farmer living beyond the yellow wastes, so he claimed, lay dying. But this farmer had heard of the Kingdom of the Lord Jesus Christ, of Paradise, where the dead Christians go and find eternal peace. Now he too would accept the True Faith before his death and be baptized. The priest's companions warned against following this servant, for they thought him little trustworthy. But Thangbrand followed the man, for his

---

19 Derogatory term for Christians among the Northmen

desire to spread the Word of God was great, and so they departed that very night. His own servants, however, the priest left back at the longhouse.

From the green meadows of the coast, they traveled further and further into the gray stony hinterland. After riding through the rocky desolation for a long while, Thangbrand's patience was wearing thin. Often he asked how much further it was. When they finally reached the edge of the yellow wastes, the serf drew his sword, ready to do the deed. But the militant Thangbrand, gruff and experienced in brawling, was not so easily killed. A fight broke out, and again and again he was able to dodge the blows and only suffered a minor flesh wound. Countless times the servant lunged at the priest, but every time he managed to parry the blow with his pack. Slowly the assassin tired, and once the priest was able to grab his sword hand, it was all over. Filled with rage and with the strength of a bear his large hands throttled the servant. The man first turned pale, then his face turned blue and his eyes bulged out of their sockets. Only after slumping to the ground in exhaustion did Thangbrand let go, but by then there was no life left in the would be murderer's body.

When the choleric man of the cloth returned to the longhouse the next day, he lay down on his bed in illness and would not get up for two full days. He evaded all the questions of his followers. Many days later the Odin worshiping farmers found the body of the servant and called upon the *thing* in Ravnswik. They publicly accused the missionary of manslaughter. But the Christian farmers defended Thangbrand, and they were able to convince the people of the priest's innocence.
But some weeks later it came to pass that a merchant from Reykjavik arrived in Eyjarfjord and recognized the

missionary of the Norwegian king. Rapidly the news spread of the manslaughter committed on the southern coast by the ill tempered man.

This time the farmers were unwilling to speak up for the priest. Some even renounced the Christian Faith. The Icelanders' anger soon rose, and Thangbrand expected to be tossed into the fjord with a stone tied around his neck. And so the only option for this most warlike man of God was to flee, just like before in Reykjavik. And so, under the cover of night and fog, he had his knarr made ready and left the island of ice together with his followers.
Thangbrand the priest of King Olaf was never seen in Iceland again.

*

5. The New World

In the late summer of the year 985 AD, Bjarni had returned to the Island of Ice after a long journey of trading in Norway. Proud of having made good profit, he returned to the farm of his father Herjulf. But there he discovered that his parents had left their Icelandic home and had followed the call of Erik Thorvaldsson, who was known as "the Red". He had once been their neighbor, but had been banished from Iceland for three years for an act of manslaughter he had committed several summers before. Following the tales of a certain Gunnbjörn who supposedly had sighted a green land far to the west, Erik had sailed along this route. And the hot-tempered Viking did indeed find Gunnbjörn's country which he hence named Greenland. He spent the three years of his exile in this new country, explored it and built a homestead which he named Brattahild.
But when the three years were up he returned to Iceland to persuade people to emigrate. And he found enough people willing to follow him.
For Iceland was a barren island and the hope for fertile lands was great among the people. And so he left the Ice Island again with twenty-five ships. But only fourteen snekkjas and knarrs survived the dangerous crossing. Having arrived in Greenland with the new settlers, Erik Thorvaldsson founded the Eastern Settlement close to his own homestead.
The farmer Herjulf who had fallen for the tales and promises of Thorvaldsson, had also decided to emigrate and followed him to Greenland.

And so Bjarni the young sailor spent the winter in the abandoned farm of his parents and went on another trading

expedition the following summer. But after his return late in the summer of 986 AD he readied his ship, which was called *Wind Horse*, to finally follow his relatives to Greenland.
"You must sail west", they had told Bjarni Herjulfsson, "Sail west until you reach a land of green meadows that reach to the shore, but with hinterlands mountainous and glaciered!"
And so Bjarni sought out a crew and set sail.

*

The sky hung grey and threatening above the North Sea and it wouldn't be long before the merciless storm broke out. The men knew this for they were experienced enough to read the signs of the sky and the sea.
But what could they do? They had sailed west far out into the open seas and there was no turning back now. The clouds billowed into black giants far too quickly and the first drops of rain drizzled onto the planks of the ships. The fat-bellied yet nimble knarr flew westwards with swollen sails and the men hoped dearly to find an island.
Bjarni had stowed the cargo away securely and lengths of rope were piled on the deck with which the men could tie themselves to the ship so they would not be swept overboard by the salty waves.
Two men wrestled with the rudder to keep *Wind Horse* on course. But the stronger the wind grew the more powerless they became. Then suddenly the storm hit them with all its might.
With her colossal paws, Ran[20] the sea goddess tossed the knarr across the waves like nutshell. But *Wind Horse* was a good ship and withstood all attempts of the cruel goddess to

---

20 Ran: dark sea goddess. She pulls sailors to her with nets and rules over the souls of the drowned. Wife of good Ægir.

crush her between her fingers. Ran raged on for nearly two days and the men were overcome with fear that they would be dragged into the sea of the dead by her nets. But then the sea calmed and the steersman regained control of *Wind Horse*. Them men thanked the sea god Ægir[21] with a sacrifice for calming his angry wife Ran.

Bjarni stood at the stern of the ship for some time, staring searchingly at the choppy sea. Then he went aft and asked the steersman: "Where do you think we are, Njal?"
Njal shrugged. "Ægir alone knows, but I believe we have sailed westward past our destination!"
Bjarni shook his head decisively. "Oh, no. The storm surely drove us eastward past Greenland", he surmised, "So the land we seek lies further to the west!"
Njal shrugged once more. "If you say so, Bjarni", he grumbled unhappily, for his sailor's pride had been wounded. And so *Wind Horse* continued westward.

The days went by without them finding their sought after land. Finally the sea had settled and a fair wind blew from the east driving the knarr swiftly before it. But how far had they strayed off course? Bjarni had lost hope of finding the green land of Erik Thorvaldsson. He wished to turn the ship around and sail east again to his home of Iceland. Perhaps he would try to follow his parents again next summer. But suddenly the man perched on the yard called out: "Land in sight!". Quickly the knarr approached the shore and Bjarni and the captain Björn stood anxious at the railing. But the closer they came the more the disappointment and certainty settled that this could not be the green land of Erik Thorvaldsson.

---

21 Ægir: good sea god who was given thanks to for calm seas. Also the god of brewing beer who would invite the other gods to drink.

The coast did not match the descriptions given to him. This land was not mountainous nor did the sailors see glaciers. Instead the country was hilly and dense green forests reached all the way down to the shore. Certainly a green and fertile land, they all agreed, but not the Greenland of Erik the Red.
For a full day they sailed north along the coast to look for the settlement of the emigrants. But all they saw were huge dense dark green forests!
Trees as far as the eye could see! Timber in great amounts to gladden the heart of any shipwright. A man could truly grow wealthy here, but that was not their goal.
Somewhat disappointed, Bjarni gave the order to change course, and so they sailed northeast out onto the open sea. And this time Ægir managed to keep his wife Ran in check for the North Sea remained calm and pleasant.
The men pulled at the oars, as Bjarni ordered, and after fewer than six days the lookout on the yard called out again. Even this far out they could already see the mighty mountains and glaciers reaching deep into the interior of the island. And then they saw the green meadows in between the rough crags reaching down to the shore.

"Yes, that must be Greenland!", Bjarni called out joyfully, and the men cheered. They sailed east along the coast and soon came upon a bay which seemed to Herjulfsson a likely spot for a settlement. And sure enough they spotted the ships of the emigrants on the beach.
Bjarni announced their arrival with a blast from his horn and dark sound answering them from shore like an echo confirmed they had been seen.
The people of the Eastern Settlement rushed out, happy to greet the new arrivals. And when *Wind Horse's* keel crunched onto the sandy beach great cheering broke out.

Men and women approached curiously. Children of all ages hopped about the beach in excitement and many helping hands pulled the ship onto land.
When Bjarni saw his father Herjulf, he knew he had reached his destination. Yes, he had finally reached Greenland! He embraced his relatives heartily and with greatest mirth, and they shed hot tears of joy, when they recognized who had come to them. He found them all in good health; his father, his mother and all his siblings who were younger than Bjarni who counted twenty summers.

"Be welcomed to the Green Island", a tall man said who approached Bjarni and his father shortly after the arrival. His hair was as red as the fire of a smith's forge and so was his long unkempt beard. This color gave the man his byname, for it was Erik Thorvaldsson himself, who was called "the Red", and he was undisputed master of the settlement. When the Red had been banished Bjarni had still been almost a boy. But the passing of years had made him, too, into a man. The son of Herjulf immediately recognized his former neighbor and greeted him politely. And he also greeted his young son Leif who had accompanied his father to the beach with a hearty handshake as was customary among men. This made the lad who was barely eleven summers and winters old puff up with pride.
Thorvaldsson counted thirty six summers and so was slightly younger than Herjulf. Yet due to his weather worn face he appeared older than his father who rarely set to sea as a farmer.
"Come to my house tonight and tell me of your crossing, Erik invited the newcomer, and he accepted gratefully.

After *Wind Horse* had been unladen, Bjarni went to his father's small farm which was not far from the settlement somewhat to the west of the bay. And here he already had to tell the saga of his journey.

When evening came they went to the home of Erik Thorvaldsson. It was located east of the settlement by a cliff, and the owner had also built for himself a mead hall. Accompanied by his father Herjulf, his captain Björn and Njal the steersman of the *Wind Horse* they soon came upon the longhouse of Erik the Red. The chieftain and *Thing* speaker of the Greenlanders feasted his guests well, and he and all his relatives listened carefully to the story of the new arrivals. They had made themselves comfortable around the great hearth at the center of the guest hall, and Erik's wife and his daughter Freydis of ten summers refilled the men's cups with beer.

Erik's oldest son Thorvald was five summers younger than Bjarni himself. Then there was Leif, the lad from the beach, and Thorstein, the youngest son who counted eight summers and winters. The stories about the land Bjarni had sighted in the west were of particular interest to the chief of the settlement. But he couldn't believe the tales of forests as far as the eye could see. He knew all too well how explorers exaggerated from his own experiences. The green land he had promised his settlers had also turned out to be less green than they had imagined. But one listener couldn't stop thinking about Bjarni Herjulfsson's stories.

*

The story of his misadventure followed Bjarni the sailor for many years. Everyone knew that the world ended in the west and that any sailors would fall off the edge of the world into the realm of the goddess Hel. Only few believed his stories and many made fun of Herjulfsson which all to often ended in quarrel. Bjarni never sailed the route west again.

His future journeys led him only to his home in Iceland and to Norway. But there was one who often still asked Bjarni about the wooded country to the west. And the elder he became, the more firmly he believed in its existence. It was Leif, the son of Erik the Red!

In the spring of 999 AD nearly fifteen years had passed since the discovery of the land to the west. Leif had become an experienced seaman and counted 24 summers and winters. Often he had sailed the North Sea on Bjarni's ship and had sailed east with him. Sometimes he attempted to persuade his father's friend to journey west. But Bjarni would not hear of it!

Then a day came when Herjulfsson lay down on a sickbed and called young Leif to his home.
"Often you have sailed with me on *Wind Horse*", he spoke as the Greenlander came nearer, "This summer it is not my lot to sail to Norway!"
Leif took a step closer and looked at Bjarni's injured leg. Careless while chopping wood had chained him to his bed.
"That looks pretty bad and must be painful", Leif said sympathetically. But he couldn't quite hide a grin at Bjarni's misfortune.
"Yes, yes", the older man grumbled at his own ineptitude, "Laugh all you want, but your ax is also sharp and your flesh soft!" The wounded sailor bore the lad's mockery with a grin for he could not stay angry at Leif.
"You have my complete trust, Leif", Bjarni said almost ceremoniously, "And that's why I want you to go trading in my stead this year!"
Leif Eriksson looked at the owner of *Wind Horse* in surprise. He had never been captain before and yet Bjarni was offering him command of his ship.

"You will be the captain and sail *Wind Horse* to Nidaras and sell my wares! Will you do this for me?", he asked.

A happy smile crossed the young seaman's face.

"Yes, Bjarni, I will do it", Leif nodded his agreement, and he could hardly contain his joy and pride. The young Greenlander was a good navigator! He could sail by the stars just as well as by a bearing plate, and he was also a good steersman. Nothing spoke against letting the young man command the journey and take responsibility for crew and ship.

Erik the Red also nodded approvingly when he heard of his son's plans.

And so in the early spring *Wind Horse* sailed out into the bay of the Eastern Settlement, heavily laden with barrels of oil and blubber, with seal hides and whale ivory. And Leif Eriksson commanded the ship that sailed out onto the North Sea.

*

It wasn't the first time Leif had gone to Norway, but he had never been to Nidaras before. Only a few summers prior had the Christian king Olaf Tryggvesson made it his royal city in the Trondheimfjord on the banks of the river Nid.

The king had had to leave the old capital of Sotenäset in the south of the country. The rebelliousness of the inhabitants of the Trøndelag had made it necessary for him to reside close by. The Trøndner had rebelled against him before. And so had had built a great fortress and port in the north of his realm. Many settlers soon followed and built dwellings alongside their king's.

Quickly Nidaras became a blossoming trade city and Leif gazed upon the beauty of the new city as the knarr entered the port of Nidaras.

"Yes, there is surely profit to be made here", he said to his steersman, who piloted *Wind Horse* with great skill to one of the many peers that extended into the bay.
But no sooner had they tied their ship up, a warrior approached the knarr.
"State your name", he said gruffly, and Leif Eriksson, who was standing at the railing, was surprised at such rudeness. "What do you want, man?", the sailor answered no less gruffly, "Is this how Norwegians greet guests to their city?". Leif took a great leap over the railing and stood directly before the guard. "My name is Leif Eriksson and I come from Greenland!"
"I hope for your sake that you're a Christian", the warrior of the city watch said, "The king only allows Christians in Nidaras!"
Leif Eriksson shook his head energetically. "No, I believe in Odin the One-Eyed and his son Thor the Hammer Bearer! In lovely Freya and good Baldr!", he spoke not without pride, "And so should you instead of praying to a slave god!"

He had heard that the King of the Norwegians was a firm believer in the new faith from the south, but that he was so blinded that he only allowed Christians in his city had been unknown to him.
"For the sake of the peace I choose to overhear your insolence", the watchman said, "But I must report your presence!" He took a step closer to Erik. "Unless you want to leave Nidaras again?"
A cheeky grin crossed his face and Leif was almost willing to draw his sword. But he kept his anger in check, not willing to squander Bjarni's faith in him. "What do you think? Go and report to your lord what there is to report!"

That same day the guard returned to the *Wind Horse*. And with ten more warriors. The Greenlandish sailors watched them assemble in amazement.

"Leif Eriksson!", the watchman called out severely, and the Greenlander stepped to the railing.

"What are you shouting about? Don't you have anything better to do?", Leif asked merrily and his men grinned from ear to ear.

"Come, the king wishes to see you", the guard commanded gruffly; he was obviously the sort of man with little sense of humor.

"The king? Is it your custom that the king should greet the traveling merchants?", Leif asked in puzzlement. Again the Greenlanders laughed and slapped their thighs.

"He must be a busy man, your king!", the steersman said with a grin.

At this the guardsman grew angry. "Are you coming, man? Or do I have to take you by force to King Olaf Tryggvesson?"

Leif gave orders to his steersman Thure, for he anticipated nothing good. And then he followed the guards to the palace. They walked through the dockland into the upper city where the wealthy merchants, the clergy and other courtly hangers-on lived. And suddenly they stood before the castle of the king.

It was a great fortress of stone and timber and several smaller buildings nearby. Surrounded by a palisade with mighty towers. The men entered the royal district through one of the gates. Leif had to wait at the doors of the great longhouse while the guard vanished inside. Only to other guards remained with the Greenlanders, the others entered one of the side buildings. Shortly the watchman returned and told Leif to enter. He allowed himself to be led inside and entered a great hall with tables and chairs lined at the sides.

"Come on, this way", the guard murmured, and the two men slowly walked forward. At the end of the hall stood the high chair of the ruler of Norway.

It was a wooden throne, ornately carved. The man who created it had been a true master, Leif thought. Near the high chair, several men were engaged in discussion, and only when they saw the newcomers did they interrupt their conversation. One of the men left the group and stood before the guard and the visitor.

"Leif Eriksson", he said with a friendly voice, and sat down on the chair. So this was Olaf Tryggvesson, Leif thought. This man who barely counted thirty summers and winters did not look like a king. At least not to the mind of Leif Eriksson the sailor. He wore a valuable but plain looking kirtle[22] embroidered with delicate silvery thread.

"It is well", the king said to the guard who bowed curtly and left. "Come closer, Leif", Tryggvesson told his guest.

"Are you the son of the Greenlander Erik Thorvaldsson?", he asked freely. Leif stared at the king in wonder. He knew his father!

"Yes, the man known as Erik the Red is my father", the Greenlander nodded.

"I would like for you to be my guest for a time, Leif", King Olaf said with a grin and an expression that struck Eriksson as odd. But to be the guest of a king was very tempting and so Leif agreed.

*

For two full moons the young Greenlander was a guest in the longhouse of the king. He had long finished his business

---

22 Kirtle: knee-length garment, commonly made of wool.

and the knarr was full of the wares bought in Norway. And Leif still had no idea of what the Norwegian king wanted of him. He had been invited into the great hall almost every evening. Had sat with the king's court at the great table and feasted with them.

Sometimes the king called on him and asked him about Greenland, the Eastern Settlement and the people who dwelt there. Often the king spoke of the salvation that the Lord Christ had granted him. And for added weight, on one evening he recited the saga of his own life. This greatly impressed Leif Eriksson, for Tryggvesson had seen much in his life, and he never forgot to praise the Lord Christ for granting him such great fortune.

Should the fortune of this new god truly be so great? Greater even than that granted by Odin?

These thoughts kept creeping into Leif's head, but he was unaware that this was the Norwegian king's design.

Then the day came when Leif Eriksson wished to take his leave of King Olaf, but he bade the Greenlander stay a while longer.

The ruler ordered his bishop to prepare a great mass for the visitor, so that he might bless Greenlander and that the Lord Christ might protect and keep him. And so it was!

On Sunday, which is the day the Christians hold their ceremonies, the entire court came to the church of Nidaras. And many common folk had come as well.

Deeply impressed by the building and the songs of the faithful, Leif sat in one of the pews of the church. He listened intently and recognized the honor when the bishop said his name. He called Leif Eriksson and asked him freely if he was ready to receive the baptism and renounce the pagan gods. And Leif agreed!

Just a few days later, Leif and his entire crew were baptized in the church of Nidaras, and the king himself was his godfather. Before his departure Tryggvesson had the young sailor promise him to spread the belief in the Lord Christ in his own lands. And to ensure this he sent a Christian priest along with him to baptize the folk of the Eastern Settlement.

*

Erik the Red was incredibly incensed that his son had brought a Christian priest back to Greenland. And many other inhabitants of the Eastern Settlement were suspicious. Many of them had fled from Norway and Iceland because of the new faith. But it didn't take long for belief in the Christian god to take root.
As so often it was the women who first took to the words and the songs of the priests. And so they were baptized. Among them was also the wife of Erik Thorvaldsson. This example let others follow them willingly, like the sons of Erik the Red, Thorvald and Thorstein. Only the Red himself and his daughter Freydis staunchly refused to receive the baptism of the Christians. But now that more than half of his family gave the Christian priests their ear, he was forced to let those of different faith be.

Finally summer came and Leif no long wished to put off his plans. So he went to the farm of Bjarni Herjulfsson.
He entered the sailor's longhouse and without many words dropped a leather pouch onto the table. Bjarni reached for it and the clinking inside betrayed the contents.
"What's this about, Leif?", Bjarni asked somewhat upset, "What should I do with this?"
"I'd like to buy your ship, old friend", said Eriksson, "This is partial payment for *Wind Horse!*"

"You want to buy *Wind Horse?* Why?", Bjarni asked surprised, for he had not expected this.
"I want to prove that your saga is true; that there is a land to the west that let's the hearts of men beat faster!"
Bjarni shook his head furiously. "Have you gone mad?"
But Leif would not be deterred. "Don't you believe what you've seen with your own eyes? Or was your story just a lie, as everyone claims?"
Bjarni remained silent.
Ever since his accident the man had not been to sea, for his wound simply would not heal properly. And since Leif's return from Norway, *Wind Horse* lay on the beach, useless. He kept silent for a while longer, in thought, but then he suddenly pounded the table with his fist.
"Give me your money! You shall have *Wind Horse!*", he shouted, laughing. The two men sat at the table into the wee hours of the night, and Bjarni Herjulfsson described once more which course Leif should take to reach the land that had brought him so much ridicule.

The next morning, Eriksson began the preparations for his long journey. With the help of some experienced men, *Wind Horse* , still lying on the beach, was overhauled. The hull was cleared of mussels and other growths and resealed with hot tar. The holes that had been gnawed in the sails by all manner of animals was carefully mended. The yard was replaced for it had rotted and the beautiful dragon head at the stern was re-carved. *Wind Horse* lay on the beach in all her new glory, seaworthy and ready to launch.
Now that all work had been done, the knarr was put to water. The great sailing ship lay tied at one of the docks that stretched into the bay of the Eastern Settlement.
And then the day that Leif Eriksson had chosen for their departure came. It was a fine summer's morning, the wind

blew coolly from the sea into the bay and the sun slowly crossed the blue sky. *Wind Horse* had been laden with everything the men would need for their voyage. Even the priest had come to the beach to bless the ship. Thus the Lord Christ would give his blessing, that the journey be successful. Leif was sure of it!

Thirty-five men had joined the son of Erik the Red and were all aboard the knarr which rocked gently on the waves. Among the Thure the skipper and Njal, who would be the steersman. He was the same as age his former captain Bjarni, with whom he had often sailed the seas, and Njal was the only one of the crew who had seen the coast of the strange land many summers and winters ago.
Now the men stood either side of the railing and in their hands they held upright the oars they would plunge into the waves as soon as the ship cast off.

Leif said goodbye to his relatives. For Erik Thorvaldsson, Lord of Greenland, and also the rest of his family would not be dissuaded from bidding him a long farewell. Almost more intimate was the farewell spoken between Leif and Bjarni, for the old man had hobbled to the peer on a crutch. He cordially embraced the man who had made this journey possible. Then Leif Eriksson was the last man to come aboard and gave the order to cast off. The oars were dropped into the water and the men sat down on their sea chests which served as their benches. Amidst great cheering of the people of the Eastern Settlement, *Wind Horse* sailed out into the fjord.

*

The skipper had decided to sail the route of Bjarni Herjulfsson from north to south and the priest's blessing seemingly was working. As the headed out beneath the shining sun, *Wind Horse* set course for the south west, propelled by a strong breeze.

The sails were swollen, the oarsmen cold pull in their oars and the ship sailed along speedily. But that would soon change!

But it was no storm that hindered their forthcoming. It was a dead calm! After three days at sea no wind blew. The great sail hang limply from the yard and the men had to put their backs into their oars. The happy mood on board quickly soured, for it had also become relatively warm. Their bodies glistening from sweat, all was silent save for the occasional groan from the exhausted men. And of course the creaking of the churning oars in their placements.

Suddenly they heard the sonorous voice of Njal the steersman. Njal had started to sing an old sailors' song, long sung by Vikings when they were at sea. It was about a beautiful wife who awaited the return of her husband, about heroic Viking deeds and Ran and Ægir the sea gods. And even though they were Christians now, none of them minded, and all sang along.

Leif who was standing aft with Thure next to Njal was surprised for he had never heard Njal sing before. Even though this was not their first voyage together. He patted him on the shoulder and shook his head laughing in disbelief.

The next morning the wind returned and drove the knarr further on, and the further they went west, the stronger the wind blew.

It was their eighth day at sea, and light rain was falling when the voice of the lookout on the yard cried out: "Land ahead! Leif Eriksson, land ahead!"

The ship quickly approached the foreign shore and the men stood curiously at the railing. But their disappointment was great when they saw the coast of the promised country.
They saw fjords surrounded by naked grey rock. And they spotted only a few meadows and forests. Could this really be the country that Bjarni Herjulfsson had spoken of?
"If I didn't know it to be impossible, I'd say that is Norway", Thure the skipper said disappointingly.
Alarmed, Leif turned to the steersman. "Njal, where are we?"
He merely shrugged. "That's certainly not the coast we saw back then", he replied stoically. The skipper gave the order to strike the sail and the man sat on their sea chests once again, oars in hand. They propelled the knarr forward with great strokes and Njal made for a bay where they might go ashore.
Quickly they made camp. The men went out to hunt and others went in search of fresh water. Soon the smell of roasting meat wafted through the campsite, and the men ate their fill, for the food at sea had been sparse. The hunters had caught a deer of a type Leif didn't recognize and a careless hare who were now both roasting on spits over the fire. There was no shortage of food at least, Leif thought, and name the land "Helluland[23]" for its bare rocks.
They remained in Helluland for several days to rest from the arduous crossing, and one morning one of the men stormed into Leif Eriksson's tent.

---

23 Helluland: „Stone Land" or „Land of flat Stones", probably Baffin Island.

"Come quickly, Leif! Come!", he cried out with excitement. The son of Red Erik groggily stood up and followed him outside. "What's all this ruckus, Thorger?", he grumbled somewhat angrily. But as he stood before the tent he was quite astonished.

"There, look!", said Thorger and pointed out into the fjord. Not far from the beach were several small boats and it seemed as if a man sat in each one. Slowly they approached the gravely shore. They were slender and pointy boats made of hide and just large enough for a single man. And Leif counted seven of them. Now the leader of the Northmen went down to the beach and with him Thure the skipper. But the boats of the natives kept a safe distance and only the one closest raised an arm in greeting. Leif returned the gesture, but the natives turned around and rowed back out into the fjord. Leif looked at Thure in puzzlement and turned around. The entire crew of *Wind Horse* had assembled behind them and some of them had drawn their weapons. Annoyed, Leif looked at the men, but said nothing. The natives did not return, against Leif's hopes, and since they had replenished their supplies, they broke camp, and rowed out of the fjord onto the open sea.

A mighty north wind blew them swiftly south. They barely had to use the oars, unless the skipper ordered them to steer into a bay or another. And the further they came south, the more the landscape changed. The craggy rocks and cliffs vanished and instead they saw huge forests.

A green canopy of leaves reached from the coast to the interior as far as the eye could see. Bjarni Herjulfsson had not exaggerated after all, and Leif Eriksson's heart sheer burst with joy. This land Leif name "Markland[24]" and after

---

24 Markland: „Wood Land", probably the coast of Labrador.

sailing along the coast for two days they found the mouth of a river.

It was a fine summer's day and the sun shone down from a cloudless sky when *Wind Horse* sailed up the river inland. On both sides of the river, dense forests and the dark green grass of sumptuous meadows reached down to the riverside. And at a point that Erik deemed suitable, they went ashore. They tied *Wind Horse* to two large trees and extended a plank across the railing.
"Yes, this must be the land that Bjarni told of", Leif exclaimed satisfied. He stood on a great meadow and the lush dense grass reached up to his knees. Surrounded by tall maple and birch woods, it was the ideal place to build a fortified camp.
"Here we will make camp and from here we will explore the country!", he slapped Thure on the shoulder. "Let's unload the *Wind Horse!*"
Soon enough the loud din of axes could be heard through the forest, their sharp blades hacking into the wood of the trees. One log at a time was brought to the meadow by the river. And as they did in their own lands, they built several longhouses with plenty of room for all the Northmen.
Here, too, there was game aplenty. Bucks and fowl, deer and hares! They had even hunted down a bear. The river was full of fat salmon, and they even found wild growing and delicious wine in large quantities.

Leif lay idly beneath one of the large trees near the camp, for it was very warm that day. "I believe I will call this land "Vinland", he mused, without looking at Thure who was dosing next to him.
"It's like that Paradise the priests are always talking about", the steersman said with closed eyes.

"Yes, that's it! I'll even call it "Vinland the Good"[25]. What do you think, Thure?"

"That doesn't sound bad", he agreed. Suddenly the name of the Norse leader echoed across the field.

"Leif! Leif!", one of the men cried and ran out of the forest. It was a young lad. His name was Kjelt and he only counted sixteen summers. He was the youngest member of the crew and a relative of Bjarni's.

Leif startled, and Thure stood up, too. "What's all this shouting?", the skipper roared angrily at the young man.

"I saw a spirit of the forest", Kjelt stammered breathlessly.

"Calm down, boy", Leif said.

"What did you see?", asked Thure, for he could not believe his ears.

"A forest spirit! I saw forest spirit!"

The two leaders looked at each other slightly amused. But they did not wish to insult him, so they let him speak.

"He looked like a man, but he was small. Much smaller than us", the young lad explained, "His skin was the color of earth and his face was red!"

"Have you gone soft in the head, Kjelt?", Thure asked and shook his head, but Leif held his arm. "Let him first speak", he ordered, and Thure fell silent.

"He was almost naked and had long black hair stuck full of feathers! You've got to believe me, Leif! It was a spirit of the forest that I saw!", Kjelt spoke almost beseechingly. "An elf or maybe even a troll! How should I know?"

"It is well, man, I believe you", Leif said to calm him, and the young lad went to the camp to tell the others of his discovery.

"You believe this nonsense?", Thure asked his leader in shock, and Leif nodded. "I've been asking myself this whole

---

[25] Vinland hit goda: „Vineland the good", probably Newfoundland.

time where the inhabitants of this fair land have been hiding".
"You mean...".
"Of course this forest spirit was a native. Remember the men from Helluland", Leif said, and Thure understood.
"Why don't they show themselves, the steersman asked. "They seem to be quite the skrælings[26]!"

But from then on the Northmen looked at the forest with watchful eyes. They moved more cautiously than they had before. And no one took so much as a step without his sword or ax close to hand.
Before winter came the men had built a large palisade around their camp. This was to protect them from raids by the natives. But none of the men saw any of these forest spirits again. The natives had vanished. And so time passed in the settlement in Vinland and soon the leaves changed color and autumn arrived. It rained often now and the wind blew strongly. But the snow fell much later than in their home, and even during the cold season, the land offered enough food to survive the winter unscathed. And as their storerooms were well filled, the Norse had no reason to fear for their well being.

Gradually it started to thaw and some of the crew started to press Eriksson to finally give the order to return. After all, they wished to see their wives again, and they had their farms to tend to.
"You have found what you sought, Leif! Now let us sail home and tell everyone the news", they said, and soon thereafter Eriksson gave in to their wish. But leaving Vinland was not easy for the Greenlander. Heavily laden with the goods of this newly discovered land they set sail at

---

[26] Skraeling: old Norse for weakling, coward.

the beginning of spring. *Wind Horse* lay deep in the water as they rowed towards the river mouth. They carried wood and the pelts of the animals they had hunted. In addition they carried wine, lots of wine which they wished to bring home to prove what Bjarni Herjulfsson had once said.

They had sailed along the coast northwards and initially the weather had been good. Rain and sunshine each took their turn and a good wind blew. But then Leif gave the order to turn north east and they sailed out onto the open sea. It would take them three days according to the reckoning of Leif and the experience of Njal to reach the waters of Greenland. And then they ran into a storm that tested the *Wind Horse* and her crew mightily.
The waves towered three men high and they made the knarr dance across their backs. But the old vessel was a good and solid ship and carried the men safely through the storm.
For a whole night the sailors fought the storm and they won. The next morning, it was already light, most of the men lay wrapped in their blankets against the railing and slept.
Only Njal, the old steersman held the rudder firmly in his strong grasp. Thure stood aft with him and looked out at the sea. Suddenly he squinted and raised his hand to shield his eyes from the sun.
"Look there, Njal", he said and pointed out to sea. Not to far out from *Wind Horse* and old boat bobbed in the water. It was a knarr and the men instantly saw she was in great need. This ship had not weathered last night's storm as well as *Wind Horse.* Her mast was broken and she was leaking. On the knarr they could also see the crew who were wildly waving to get their attention. Fifteen people did they take aboard before the ship finally sank beneath the dark waves. They were emigrants from Iceland on their way to the settlement of Erik the Red. Leif praised the Lord Christ for

granting him such blessing and the saved gave him the byname "inn heppni", the Fortunate.

Soon thereafter, the *Wind Horse* reached the fjord of the Eastern Settlement. The signal horn from the cliffs heralded their arrival and the inhabitants flocked to the beach.
The joy at their arrival was great and many hands slapped the shoulders of the homecomers. And they were astonished at the wares Eriksson presented from the country they had discovered. But the one who was the most please at Leif Eriksson's return was old Bjarni. He had come to the beach on his crutch and embraced the young sailor, as if he were his own son. Finally he had proven that the land to the west existed and no one would dare ridicule Bjarni Herjulfsson again.

*

A few years later, Thorvald, Leif's elder brother equipped his ship to sail to Vinland. He had seen how heavily laden his brother's ship had returned, and the wealth of the country enticed him. So he attempted the crossing and arrived unharmed on coast of the land that his brother had named Vinland hit goda. They even found the bay where Leif had landed and the camp he had built. They lived in the fort which they expanded to a village for two winters without incident, until one morning they came across men for the first time. Three small boats made of hide rowed towards the beach. Nine men, small of stature with bronzed skin and black hair sat in them. They were armed with knives and spears when they set foot on the beach.

But Thorvald was hot-tempered and violent like his father Erik the Red. Unfortunately he did not have his father's intelligence and attacked the strangers. With their swords and axes the Norse killed eight of the natives and only one managed to escape. This one returned to the bay a short time later and with him a vast fleet of boats. Without hesitation the brown-skinned men whose faces were now painted red attacked strange invaders. A hail of arrows rained down on the Greenlanders and after a fierce battle that cost many attackers their lives, the Norse retreated to their longhouses. They had beaten back the overwhelming numbers of the natives, for they vanished into the bay in their hide boats. But Thorvald Eriksson had been hit by arrows and died the same day. After the eldest son of Erik the Red had found his grave in Vinland, the other Northmen decided to return to Greenland. But again their ship was filled to the brim when they reached their home shores, and it would not be the last Norse expedition to Vinland.

*

6. ALFRED THE GREAT

Twenty-three years of age was Alfred the Anglo-Saxon when he stood by the sick bed of his elder brother Aethelred I in 871 AD.
Together they had fought a great battle. The first battle against the great invading army of Vikings in Wessex. But now the king lay dying and Alfred knew that which he had dreaded all his life was about to happen. He who had wished to live a life behind abbey walls, he who was already a novice, should sit on the thrown of Wessex by will of the councilors. And as much as he wished it weren't so, he knew that this was his destiny.

*

It was on a morning during the last days of August when the Viking ships plowed through the early fog that lay on the water before the shores of Wessex. Fearsome dragon heads were carved into the sterns of the slender *snekkjas* bobbed with the rhythm of the waves and quickly approached the beach. Most of the folk in the nearby village were still fast asleep when the keels of the ships crunched against the sandy shore.
For several years now these Vikings had ravaged the island of the Anglo-Saxons. They had already conquered the kingdoms of Northumbria, Mercia and East Anglia. The kings and their retainers had either been killed or put to flight. And since most of the Vikings were Danes, they named the conquered land the *Danelaw*.
The Saxon population of these petty-kingdoms had been driven off, killed or enslaved and in their place came

Danish, Swedish and Norwegian settlers. They then claimed the farms, towns and cities of the Saxons for their own. And so the host of Northmen went from one coast of Britain to the next raiding, plundering and killing, and few kings were able to resist them with force of arms.

Now the Kingdom of Wessex under Aethelred I was to be their victim, for they constantly sought new spoils and land. Many sea-kings and jarls led the great army and every one of them wanted his share of the plunder.
A portion of the northern warriors began their bloody work and attacked the sleeping village immediately. Few people managed to escape into the vast forests that sprawled from the outskirts of the settlements deep into the countryside. The other Vikings heaved their ships ashore so that they were strewn across the beach like pearls on a string. Then they built a great camp in which many fires were lit and one tent was pitched next to the other. Only a handful of warriors made their quarters in the abandoned village for fear of the fleas and lice there. They preferred to sleep in their tents. The largest tent was occupied by the chief warlord of the Vikings. A Danish sea-king, and as long as he was successful he would not have to worry about his leadership.

Soon the news of the arrival of the Viking host had reached King Aethelred's court and shortly afterwards, messengers of the Northmen were sent to the king and demanded a ransom. Aethelred asked for time to consider this proposal and the messenger agreed.
"But do not take too long, King of Wessex", the warrior who was certainly a jarl warned, "That could be bad for you and your subjects!" And with a brash grin he and his companions retired.

The king called on his councilors to discuss the dire situation. Some of his courtiers urged him to pay the sum, even though it was high and would have emptied the coffers to their very bottom. Others wished to fight the invaders. "If we pay them off now they will only attack us again next year", said a man by the name of Alfey who was an earl. Many agreed with him. "Our army is not strong enough to fight these heathen devils", another cried. The king looked to his brother Alfred whom he had summoned. Aethelred always listened to the council of his younger brother for he himself was sickly and not of any great strength. Furthermore, Alfred was well read due to his time spent in the monastery, and men said he was cunning.
"What do you say, Alfred?", Aethelred asked his brother. The young man raised his shorn head. "Do you ask me as a man of God or as the brother of the king?"
"Is there a difference?", Aethelred asked in puzzlement.
"Oh, indeed there is. As a man of God, I must tell you to give them the money."
Those who were in agreement nodded, pleased that the king's brother was also of this opinion. The other men looked angry. "But as the king's brother I say Alfey is right! Next year these raiders will return, and so I think it better to face them sword in hand!"
"But our army is not strong enough", the king answered, "The pagans will overrun us!"
The men agreed with their lord, for even though some were willing to fight, they did not wish to sacrifice their men needlessly. Alfred kept silent for a long time.
"If the enemy is too strong, then perhaps cunning can help us", he suddenly said. The men listened eagerly.
"We shall send two armies to the battlefield which will attack the Vikings at the same time! This way they will not know which enemy to attack!"

The king nodded his agreement. "So it shall be done. I will lead the first army, and you the second, my brother!"
"Me?", Alfred cried out in alarm, "No, I am a man of the cloth!"
But Aethelred gew angry. "You will lead the army", he said gravely, "In these dire times you are no longer a novice, but the brother of the King of Wessex! It is your duty to fight for our people!"
But now Alfred was stubborn and left in a huff. Only after the bishop of Wessex implored him to comply did he reluctantly agree to the plan. Aethelred told the messenger of the Vikings that the invaders were to leave peacefully, otherwise they would face the pagans with swords drawn and toss them back into the sea, by the power of the Lord Jesus Christ.

*

A single large thorn tree stood on a hill where the Viking host had assembled, and here the armies were to meet. Not far from the hill a road lead off to the west to the town of Ashdown. Down this road marched the army of the Saxons lead by the king's brother Alfred, and Aethelred was to join the battle with his army from the north.
Slowly Alfred's army made for the base of the hill and set up a defensive position. But there was no sign of Aethelred's army.
When the Viking king saw how small the Saxon army was he began to laugh and ordered his men to attack. With his sword held high he charged in at the head of his warriors. And not even the hail of arrows raining down upon them was enough to dissuade the warriors of the north.
The Vikings smashed into the lines of the Saxons, but the defenders stood firm. Sword and axe blades left deep gashes

in the flesh of the combatants. Spear points were thrust deep into bodies and bones burst. Then a horn sounded out and the Northmen withdrew with their wounded to the top of the hill. Alfred's army, too, regrouped and tended to the wounded. Many corpses remained strewn across the field and were soon a feast for crows. But it was not long before the name of Odin was bellowed by hundreds of voices and the Vikings stormed down the hill once more.

Again and again the northern warriors attack the Saxons at the foot of the hill without mercy or regard for their own lives. And by midday the host of Alfred had been dangerously decimated. But finally, when the Saxons and their chieftains had nearly lost hope, the army of Aethelred marched onto the battlefield.

The men fought on with renewed courage, and when the Viking king fell dead to the ground, pierced by many spears, the attackers retreated. The Northmen had lost their king and five jarls and for the first time had been defeated on Saxon soil.

But King Aethelred also was not unscathed. A spear had wounded him and as he was not particularly strong to begin with and often sick, the healers soon gave up on him. Alfred came to his sick bed of the dying man who made him promise to become his successor and King of Wessex. The following night the king's brother was summoned again to Aethelred's bedside. The closest courtiers and the bishop were gathered there in the light of the candles. Alfred approached the bed, sank to his knees and began to pray. Aethelred, the King of Wessex was dead!

And so the day had come on which Alfred had to take his brother's place and rule the country. The line of blood demanded he succeed his brother, for Aethelred had sired no children. But often this man, red of hair, who now had to be king, sat in a small chamber of the abbey, reading in old tomes and books.

*

The Vikings entrenched themselves on the shores of Wessex and built a great camp and did not appear to want to leave. This would have meant acknowledging defeat. From here they launched raids into the interior and sometimes they sent messengers to King Alfred's court demanding tribute. This appeared to happen whenever the Northmen chose a new leader at a *thing*. If a leader had seemingly run out of luck, he had lost the favor of the gods, and was in danger of being replaced by another jarl or captain.

Since King Alfred refused to pay tribute, battles were fought repeatedly, but with no clear victor. No Viking king or jarl was capable of toppling the young Saxon from his throne. And so it came to pass that the Vikings yet again elected a new warlord. He was a Dane named Guthrum and not much older than the King of Wessex himself.

Guthrum also sent demands which were refused and fighting broke out anew. But again, Alfred was able to defeat the attackers, who angrily went on to ravage the countryside. The folk in the villages and farms suffered greatly at their hands and so they told the king of their plight. Alfred promised to do all in his power to make the heathens pay for their crimes.

He assembled the last of his forces and drove the savage hordes back to the coast. But now his army was so small that he had no hope of resisting any further attacks. If Guthrum had marched on King Alfred again, he would surely have lost his crown, for the numbers of the Northmen were still great. But fortune was on the side of the Saxons,

for Guthrum, the Viking king retired to his fortified camp. The Vikings licked their wounds and waited.
Finally winter came and with it peace, for there was seldom fighting during the cold season.

Some years passed, and the battles between the Saxons of Alfred and the Vikings of Guthrum became fewer. King Alfred had taken the daughter of one of his ealdormen, whom he had known since childhood, as a bride. And soon she had given him a son. At last the king had come to know happy times.
Open conflicts with Guthrum's warriors were rare for the Kingdom of Wessex was now effectively divided. The interior was ruled by Alfred. The borderlands were in the hands of the Vikings who limited themselves to raids in the neighboring Saxon lands.

One day, it was during the spring of 978 AD, a messenger once again arrived at the court of King Alfred. A meeting was to take place between the two rulers. Guthtum wished to look the king in the eye as he made his demands known, for it would be about nothing less than Alfred's very crown. The jarls and ship captains were unhappy, for they had come to conquer the land, not devastate it. They wished to expand the borders of the Danelaw and create a great Nordic kingdom. The petty raids satisfied them no longer.
Rumors were whispered that the gods had deserted Guthrum and it would be better to elect a new leader. Guthrum's position was precarious and he was forced to act. The Dane knew only the complete conquest of Wessex or a great amount of money thrown at the feet of his jarls would save his rule.
With only a small number of retainers, the kings met near Edington. A tent had been erected on an open field, in which

the rulers would sit opposite one another in their high seats. A few councilors, marshals, jarls and chieftains stood behind their kings.

"My army is larger and braver than yours, Saxon", Guthrum growled menacingly, "It would be child's play for us to overwhelm you, King of Wessex!"

"So why have you not already don so, Viking?", Alfred asked unimpressed. "I shall tell you why. Because you can't".

At this the Viking king burst out laughing. "Every summer new ship crews from the Danelaw join my army. How long do you think you can stand against our numbers?"

This arrogant statement opened the Saxon king's eyes. Alfred understood that if he delayed any longer, the army of Vikings would only grow larger and larger. This was the reason, why there had been no further attacks. The Northmen were massing their forces for one final decisive battle in which Alfred would lose his crown and country.

"But one should not butcher a cow one wishes to milk...", Guthrum looked at the Saxon brashly. "Pay me eight thousand pounds of silver and you shall have two summers of peace!"

Alfred's retainers cried out for this was an impudent demand. But Alfred called them to order. Guthrum seemed to read the thoughts of his counterpart.

"If you think you can raise an army during this time, you are sorely mistaken, Christian!" The blonde Dane stared at the King of Wessex with piercing eyes. "You will of course give me a hostage of my choosing", he proclaimed, as if he were a lord and Alfred his vassal.

"And who can assure me that you will honor this agreement, heathen?", Alfred responded coldly.

"I too, will give you a hostage! See here, this is my brother!" Guthrum laughed out loud and gestured to a man behind his chair. The man giggled childishly, and while he bore weapons and armor, under his armed he carried a wooden horse, and his eyes showed that he indeed had the mind of a child.

King Alfred asked time for consideration, and Guthrum agreed. The kings both returned to their camps.

A few days later they met again and Guthrum asked, if Alfred accepted his demands and conditions.

"For the sake of peace and because my councilors urge it, I will accept your conditions", Alfred answered, "But instead of eight thousand pounds of silver, I can only pay you six thousand".

The Viking considered this briefly, ran his fingers through his blonde beard and gave him a wicked grin. "Good! So it shall be done!"

"And now I will name the hostage I have chosen!" Guthrum sat back in his high seat. "I choose your wife, Alfred! Send me your queen and you will have two summers of peace!"

Now the Saxons protested. And Alfred angrily sprung up from his beautifully carved seat.

"Are you mad, Northman?", he roared, "That is shameless demand, and you will pay with your blood for it!".

Now the councilors had their hands full trying to prevent a fight between the two kings.

"Here at this very spot you shall pay for your insults, heathen!", Alfred shouted as he pulled the tent flap aside. He pointed at a large field that lay between a dense forest and a marsh. "Here I will assemble my army, and if you have the courage you will face me, yellowbeard!"

"You're mad, Saxon", Guthrum mocked the King of Wessex calmly. "Just as mad as my brother here", he pointed to the young man playing with a child's rattle. "But if that is your wish it shall be done!"

The negotiations were ended and the kings returned to their keeps.

*

Morning mist lay over the great meadow and swamp near Edington. It was summer but the sun was hidden by thick grey clouds heavy with rain. Every now and then, drops of rain dripped onto the ground which was the camp site of Alfred's army. But this played into the strategy that he had designed for the battle. The king had retired to an abbey after the meeting with Gurhrum. Here he pored over ancient books and chronicles until he finally found what he was looking for. It was a book that spoke of the military knowledge of the Romans, and Alfred chose an ancient defensive tactic that should prove useful against the Northmen.

It was around midday when broke camp and made for the battlefield Alfred had chosen. Now the dark cloud cover had receded and rays of sunlight began to warm the ground, causing the dampness to rise into the air in wisps of mist. For now the enemy was no where to be seen, but that would soon change!

They could hear them singing in the distance, and the sound of their dark hoarse voices startled the Saxons, for the enemy was advancing. Led by their king, Guthrum the Dane. Bearing their round shields before them and clutching their sharp axes, swords and spears, the warriors of the north marched towards the Saxon host singing. Alfred shouted out his orders and the English warriors assumed the old Roman defensive formation.

The Vikings came within arrow's reach, then they paused. The singing of the Northmen ceased and for a moment it was still as a grave.

Guthrum raised his sword and bellowed the name of the Nordic father of gods. "Odin!", his warriors echoed him in their thousands. Many a Saxon felt his innards turn to ice and some of the younger warriors, who had never seen battle before, felt their own piss trickling down their legs. With fearsome war cries the Vikings charged down the gentle hill against their enemies and crashed into a wall of shields and bodies with terrible force.

The defenders stabbed at the Northmen with spears and swords, who swung wildly with their axes at the fortress of shields. Some of the more daring Vikings were the first to enter Valhalla and sit at Odin's table. Again and again, Alfred and his captains ordered the men to hold the line and not take one step back. Any Saxon, who foolhardily attempted to leave the safety of the shield wall and fight the Northmen man to man was quickly dispatched by the attackers. The Vikings attacked the wall of men for some time until eventually a horn signal was given and they withdrew from Alfred's shield wall. But it did not take long for them to regroup and the enemy from the north attacked once again. But for now the ring of Saxon defenders was holding. Every fallen English warrior was replaced with another from the second rank and after every Viking assault, the army of the King of Wessex was diminished. The shield wall melted like butter on a hot summer's day, and though the attacking army also suffered horrible losses, it seemed as their overwhelming numbers would eventually carry the day. The courage of the younger warriors left them. And even the veterans of Alfred's army knew only a divine miracle could save their skins. Alfred, caked in blood at the center of his warriors was fighting for his crown and country and urged the men to stand strong. After one last attack, the warriors of Guthrum finally withdrew. Soon the evening darkness would give them a respite, Alfred knew, but what would happen tomorrow? Should they run from the battlefield under the cover of darkness like thieves in the night? Then his crown would be forfeit and his people would be the slaves of the Northmen or worse, all killed. No! This could not be the fate that the Lord God had chosen for the King of Wessex. Alfred sat on a large stone, lost in thought, staring into the faces of the battered men around him.

"Pardon me, my lord!", a bright voice spoke out and pulled the king out of his reverie. A young lad with red hair and large freckles, surely no older than sixteen years, stood before him.

"My name is Kain Barrow, and I know this place well. I grew up hear and used to play in the marsh as a boy!", he pointed out into the darkness and Alfred did not doubt that the marsh lay in that direction.

"In the middle of the moor, there's a small patch of solid ground, large enough for a small army!"

The young lad started to grin and Alfred understood. "Tell me, Kain Barrow, could you find your way there even in the darkness?"

"King Alfred, I know this swamp as well as the chamber of my father's mill that I live in", he said proudly. Alfred put his hand on the boy's shoulder. "You are as cunning as a fox, soldier! If we should survive the day, I will reward you for this!"

Led by the miller's boy and under the cover of night, the entire army of Wessex ventured into the impassable marsh and positioned themselves on the patch of solid ground at the center. The next morning, when one of the Viking warriors told Guthrum that the Saxons had vanished, he was most surprised.

Guthrum was unsure: Should he laugh at Alfred's cowardice or be angry for being robbed of his victory. But at midday one of the warriors came to him and said he had spotted the Saxons in the swamp while hunting for grouse. Immediately Guthrum called for his warriors and marched straight into the marsh. But the soft treacherous ground made it difficult for the Vikings to reach the Saxon shield wall, and some of the older, seasoned warriors knew what was coming. It was as if the Christian God finally decided to show the Saxons mercy, and to the chagrin of the Northmen, the skies opened up and heavy rain began to fall. The water rose up to the Vikings knees and they were bogged down in the mire. It was hard going for the Northmen, but Guthrum drove his warriors on. As the jarls started to grumbled he blamed them and their avarice as the true cause for this battle. He would have been content to rule the borderlands of Wessex. And so the ship captains held their tongues and fought.

Now the situation for the army of Wessex had improved considerably. The first attack of Guthrum's Vikings was fought with ferocity and blood lust, once they reached the solid ground in front of the Saxon shield wall. But it soon became clear that the attackers were quickly tiring. They had gone through a grueling march through the swamp, and were forced to do so again, every time they withdrew and regrouped. They were weakened and soon lost the will to fight when they saw that many of their comrades were dying a dishonorable death by sinking into the depths of the swamp. The next attack of the Vikings was much more reluctant, much to the anger of their king. Alfred understood the situation and the Saxons fought the attackers mercilessly and killed many. The morale of the Northmen was utterly broken. Their advantage in numbers was gone, and they retreated back to the great meadow where the battle had begun. King Alfred of Wessex pursued them with his army, and when the Vikings finally reached solid ground, they were faced by a peasant army, which had gathered there. Armed with scythes and pitchforks, the folk had come together to drive the invaders from their land for good. When Guthrum saw this he gave the order to retreat back to their great encampment on the borders of Wessex.

There was much rejoicing among the people, and Alfred knew what had to be done. He gathered his warriors once more and replenished the ranks with the bravest of the peasants. And so he marched to the borders of his land, where the Northmen ruled and set siege to Guthrum's fort. And at last, two weeks after the Battle of Edington, Guthrum accepted defeat.

He fell on his knees before Alfred and declared he would leave the Kingdom of Wessex. But before leading his army back to East Anglia, he was baptized and took the name of Aethelstan.

In the years to come, Alfred did all in his power to reclaim the lands of the Danelaw for the Saxons. In the year 885 AD he was able to drive the Northmen from the area around London and the people gave him the by-name "the Great". The fleet he then built to protect the coasts from the Viking raids is considered to this day to be the foundation of the Royal Navy.

*

7. The Battle of Hjörungafjord

The monks recorded the year 986 AD when in the great realm of the Danes, ruled by Harald Bluetooth, his illegitimate son Sweyn rebelled against him, and a brutal civil war broke out for the rulership of the Daneland.
King Harald had already seen more than fifty summers and winters, and when he had succeeded his father Gorm many years ago, the counties of Denmark had been united into a great kingdom. But since Harald had embraced the faith of the Christians and had brought many missionaries into the land, his son Sweyn and some of the counties rebelled against the king. He was, as were many of the Danish folk, fervent followers of the god Odin and all the gods that ruled the fates of men from Asgard. Now he wished to fight for his inheritance. And so it came to open war between the father and the son whom he had sired with a maidservant. Thus Sweyn assembled his warriors and mustered a large fleet.
Autumn had already arrived when the decisive battle was fought for the Danish crown off the island of Bornholm, and the son emerged victorious. But Harald Bluetooth was grievously wounded in battle by an arrow and taken away by the former foster father of the young Sweyn, a jarl by the name of Palnatoki.

*

In the land of the Pomeranians and Slavs in the area known as Jom which had been conquered by the Danes from the Poles was a great castle, not far from the mouth of the Oder. Built many years ago by the Danish Vikings to guard the

Pommeranian conquests, the fortress towered over the flat coastlands. Large and formidable was this castle and the walled harbor boasted space for three hundred ships. Here lived and ruled the Jomsvikings. A band of men, similar to a knightly order, these warriors lived according to strict rules that they followed unconditionally. No Jomsviking was younger than eighteen or older than fifty and all swore an oath to never show fear or flee from battle. If any of them wished to lay with a woman he had to do so outside the castle walls, for women were not welcome at the Jomsburg. But no Viking was permitted to leave the castle for more than three days. And each of them had also sworn to avenge his fallen comrades. And this was the case even after men left the ranks of the Jomsvikings for they felt bound to this oath for life. The fortress and especially the reputation of its occupants was so fearsome that few warlords dared assault the Jomsburg. And in the shadow of the castle a town had quickly sprung up which the Poles called Jumne that became a flourishing trade city.

Danes and Swedes and all tribes from the realm of the German emperor, Slavs and merchants from the realm of Kiev, even Greeks and Arabs came to trade in Jumne. They did not mind the tribute they had to pay to the jarl of Jomsburg, for here they were safe from predations. Thanks to this tribute and their regular raiding the coffers of the castle were well filled and even though the Danish king saw the Vikings in Poland as his subjects, they were in truth long independent of any ruler. And so the Palnatoki of Funen, the jarl of Jomsburg, ruled as a lord over Pomerania.

It was autumn and the wind wipped the waves of the Baltic Sea when the ships arrived at the narrow channel between Wolin and Usedom. They crossed the Oder Lagoon and soon saw the towers and walls of their keep. To this place the jarl brought the badly wounded king Harald Bluetooth.

But just a few days after the former King of the Danes died of his injuries. Jarl Palnatoki paid his king his last respects and even brought a Christian priest to bury him according to his wishes. The ruling jarl and all the Jomsvikings were fervent followers of the Aesir and Odin was their chief warlord to whom they prayed and brought their bloody sacrifices. They would never let themselves be sprinkled in Holy Water and buried in the cold earth like a dead dog. No, they would die in battle sword in hand. They would be given to the flames and led by Valkyries, the beautiful daughters of Odin to Valhalla to drink of the draught of oblivion at the table of the Father of the Gods. Thus all the burden carried by the warriors of Midgard would be taken away.

But when the new King of the Danes Sweyn Haraldson, who called himself Forkbeard heard that his father had died in the Jomsburg, he prepared a feast in Roskilde and invited Jarl Palnatoki. Now a councilor of the king who was enemy to Palnatoki passed an arrow around and asked, if any man recognized it as his. Palnatoki stood and said that it had been him who had loosed the arrow at King Harald. King Sweyn was most angered by this and Jarl Palnatoki and his companions had much difficulty in leaving Roskilde unharmed and returning to the Jomsburg.

Harald dared not undertake a punitive strike against the Jomsvikings. But the deed of his erstwhile foster father had shown him that his command over the county of Jom was limited. They did not belong to the army of the King! They were and remained free warriors who acted on their own will.

During those days King Sweyn had a larger problem besides the Jomsvikings. For after the death of Harald the tributary Norwegian kings and jarls who were his vassals threatened to revolt and deny him the taxes he so desperately needed. At the head of this revolt was Jarl Hakon Sigurdson, the jar of Lade at the mouth of the river Nid on the great Trondheimfjord. Hakon had proclaimed himself King of Trøndelag in northwestern Norway, even though he had been a vassal of King Harald Bluetooth. But not that Harald Gormsson was no longer among the living he had seen the time come to rid himself of the Danish oppressors. In the autumn he expelled the royal tax collectors of Sweyn Forkbeard and proclaimed himself sole ruler of all of western Norway and that he would not pay tribute to Denmark. This angered King Sweyn so greatly that he could only entertain a single thought: to force the renegade Norwegian jarl back under his rule.

But the spring of 987 AD the army of the Danish King was still in a sorry state. The civil war against his father had cost many warriors their lives and the king had little trust in those men who had once sworn allegiance to his father. And so in the spring he sent a messenger to the Jomsburg who was to persude Jarl Palnatoki of Funen to put the Vikings of the Oder under Sweyn Forkbeard's command and sail with him to Norway to punish the renegade Jarl Hakon of Lade. But the jarl of Jomsburg knew of the reputation of the Trøndners from experience.
Often the Jomsvikings had gotten a bloody nose from raiding in the Trøndelag. These were enemies to be taken seriously. Often unruly towards their rulers, but true and steadfast in their oaths. Brave and merciless towards their enemies and always ready for battle. So Palnatoki asked the man what gain the Jomsvikings would have of this. But Sweyn's messenger was poor with words and answered this would be a journey to war and not to personal gain. There would be little to gain but glory and reputation. And of course the honor of serving the King of Denmark!

The jarl laughed heartily at this and said that oft times he had tanned the hide the king when he had been disobedient, and without him he would never have become king in the first place. After this some of the jarl's captains suggested drowning the messenger in the Oder. At least then he would provide a bit of amusement.

But Jarl Palnatoki let him leave in peace and King Sweyn was not at all pleased by the results of this parley. He knew all too well that he would need the help of the Oder Vikings to conquer Trøndelag. And so he journeyed to Pomerania himself. He sailed across the Baltic Sea with fifteen longships and when he came to the Jomsburg a messenger was sent ahead to announce his presence. But only after Jarl Palnatoki had promised guest right and free passage did the ships row into the harbor. King Sweyn was received by the leader of the Jomsvikings and all his leading jarls with proper honor. And King Sweyn thanked the jarl of Jomsburg for it.

That very day the first negotiations took place which were adjourned without results. So Sweyn approached his foster father Palnatoki and suggested they have a great feast. This would surely loosen the tension and the parties would quickly come to an agreement. This suggestion was accepted by the jarls and Palnatoki ordered there be a celebration in the Jomsburg and Jumne in honor of the king. Only one warned Palnatoki against his foster son. A jarl named Sigvaldi. For who knew if he had forgiven him for the arrow that had killed his father? In the evening the chief jarls of the Jomsvikings and the king sat together at the table and feasted. Meat and bread were set before them and the mead and beer flowed freely. Some of the men were soon in their cups, among them young Vagn of only twenty summers and winters, and of whom they said that he had captained his own ship at the age of twelve. The mood became more and more boisterous and the men more and more drunk. And now it was seen that the King of the Danes was not nearly as drunk as he had let the jarls believe. He reproached the Jomsvikings with killing Harald Bluetooth and reminded Palnatoki that he and many of his men were Danes and thus should swear fealty to him. But gracious as he was, he was willing to forgive them their misconduct and forget about the dispute with his foster father. They only had to prove to him that he could count on the men of the Oder. Drunkenly the men cheered their new king and promised to be good subjects for many of them still had relatives in Denmark and they wanted to spare them any trouble with Sweyn. The king pretended to think hard on how the Jomsvikings could prove their loyalty and soon he had thought up a solution: the Jomsvikings would drive Jarl Hakon Sigurdsson out of the Trøndelag. "Yes, that would be adequate proof", thought Sweyn. "Or was it possible that the great Jomsvikings were afraid?"

This remark led to much outrage and the men agreed to the plan indignantly. Now Sweyn raised his mead horn as well and drank contently. He had accomplished more than he had hoped, for now the Jomsvikings would attack Trøndelag alone without his Danish warriors. It hadn't been that difficult at all to outsmart the old Jarl Palnatoki.

*

The hangover was great the next morning. And the chief jarls of Sweyn's foster father became painfully aware of what they had drunkenly promised. But there was no turning back if they didn't want to lose face. They were the Jomsvikings after all!

Feared throughout the North and in all other kingdoms. If they were to be accused of cowardice the Jomsburg itself would be in danger. And so they grudgingly had to keep their promise to Sweyn and conquer the land of Hakon Sigurdsson for him. The resentment of Sweyn Forkbeard was great among the ship captains for they realized their leaders had been tricked. But none dared speak out. A few days later Forkbeard left the Jombsburg quite satisfied and returned to Roskilde, the King's city in Denmark. But not without reminding the leader of the Oder Vikings of his oath. Offended and slightly upset old Palnatoki bade his foster son farewell, but vowed to keep fulfill his promise this very summer.

Soon thereafter preparations were maid in the Jomsburg and all the county for the upcoming war in Norway. Every captain was responsible for readying his snekja and all the warriors under his command. But since Jumne was a large and busy trading port, there were also merchants from Trøndelag in Pomerania. And before long rumors were heard of a planned attack of the Jomsvikings on Norway. Soon every inhabitant and every traveler in the town knew where the wrath of the Jomsvikings was headed. And all whispered of the ruse of Sweyn Forkbeard to trick the jarls. Thus it came to pass that Norwegian merchants brought the news of the impending invasion of the Jomsvikings to Trøndelag, to the court of Jarl Hakon Sigurdsson.

And then summer came and the fleet of the Vikings of Jom sailed down the Oder and out into the Baltic Sea. Only thirty ships worth of men did Jarl Palnatoki leave behind in the Jombsburg. They were to defend the keep should the Polish king seek to gain control of the county of Jom. But a fleet of more than one hundred and twenty ships set sail for Norway. They sailed cross the great sound of Denmark until the reached the Norwegian county of Hardanger. The fleet sailed past the cape and trading port of Lindesnes and set course for the north. Soon afterwards the ships reached the entrance to the great Fjord of Trondheim. But as the many warships and dragon boats headed for the shore of Lade they were greeted by the large army of Jarl Hakon. News of the enemy fleet's departure had reached the jarl of the Trønders early. And so he had enough time to send the arrow of war from one farm and homestead to the next to assemble all the men in his domain into an army. When the first ships of the warriors of Jomsburg landed on a beach near the mouth of the river Nid, the war of the Vikings had began! Barely had the warriors of the Oder pulled the keels of their ships ashore when the jarl of Lade led the first attack. The battle was wild and fierce and soon the beach ran red with the blood of the dead and dying. But more and more ships made it to the shore, and Hakon Sigurdsson was forced to withdraw if he did not wish to lose the war in the first days. Jarl Palnatoki had the men build a great camp from which he would direct the battles. His captains assembled their warrior bands, mostly five to ten ships' crews and went to battle as old Palnatoki told them to.

On a large open meadow the armies of the brothers Sigvaldi and Thorkell the High were the first to meet a band of warriors of the jarl of Lade and a fierce battle was fought that lasted two full days. Only after a ferocious fight were the Trøndners vanquished and left the field to their enemies. On other fronts the armies of Hakon were more successful. The Trøndners were able to defeat a large muster of Jomsvikings and take their leaders as prisoners. Among them young Vagn of Viken and Björn the Welshman. Soon afterwards however the tides of battle turned against Jarl Hakon and the Jomsvikings gained the upper hand. Few battles went in his favor and every day it seemed more likely he would lose control of the Trøndelag. Now he believed that the gods had forsaken him and taken their favor from him. And when his desperation was greatest and the warriors threatened to abandon him, a gothi came before the ruler of Trøndelag. He claimed to have received a sign from the goddesses Thorgred and Irpa in which they demanded a sacrifice. He said since Hakon demanded something great, namely lordship over Trøndelag, he must offer something dear to him. Then surely the gods would restore their favor to him and he would drive the Jomsvikings from the land. Long did the self proclaimed king think on the words of the gothi and one evening, while sitting in his longhouse with his family and some trusted friends he jumped to his feet. He grabbed the arm of his son Erling who was only seven summers old and pulled him none too gently out of the longhouse out into the darkness. Silently the others looked at one another but none spoke. A small eternity later Hakon Sigurdsson returned. He came alone and his hands were drenched in blood.

*

Soon after the fortune of war changed yet again and returned to the Trøndnerjarl. Victory after victory was won against the superiority of the Jomsvikings, and Hakon was convinced his sacrifice had pleased the gods and brought them back to his side. Now the forces of the Trøndners managed to push the Jomsvikings hard enough to force Palnatoki to abandon his camp and seek refuge in a small bay close to the Trondheimfjord.
But he would not abandon his endeavor of taking Trøndelag for King Sweyn. At Hjörungafjord he mustered his Viking army once again to do battle with Hakon. But this time he was too quick for the old jarl. With an army advancing on

land and a strong fleet on the waters the Trøndners attacked the bay. Without hesitation the warriors of Hakon fell upon the invaders of the Danish king and a merciless battle ensued. Jarl Hakon threw all of his men into battle for who could say how long his gods would favor him? The army on the shore quickly managed to overrun the encampment of the Jomsvikings, for the surprise of the warriors from the Oder was great. And so the battle was lost for them and many brave men found their bloody deaths. The chieftains of the Jomsvikings were force to acknowledge their defeat in the face of the Trøndners stubbornness. The leading jarls implored Palnatoki to finally give up this endeavor. For if all the warriors were to die in the north, the Jomsburg would be defenseless against her enemies. And so the Vikings made for their ships and sailed out into the fjord. But there the fleet of the jarl of Lade lay in wait and the bloody fighting continued. Now finally the chief captain of the Jomsvikings blew into his horn to sound the retreat and the fleet sailed out of Hjörungafjord onto the open sea. The attempt to conquer Trøndelag for King Sweyn Forkbeard had failed and had cost the Jomsvikings many warriors. Most of the prisoners captured by Jarl Hakon were put to death. But the Jomsvikings showed great courage even as their end approached. Indifferent and undaunted they made fun of the executioner. And every one of them had a rhyming taunt on his limps when the sword fell. Only gray Björn and young Vagn found a way to outsmart the executioner. Björn through himself against the man and Vagn grabbed the sword. A mighty blow felled the man, and Erik Hakonsson, the eldest son of the Trøndnerjarl spared the lives of these two brave Jomsvikings.

Four years passed during which Sweyn Forkbeard ruled Denmark and tried to expand the borders of his realm.

Particularly the petty-kings of southern Norway suffered under his greed for land, and soon they too were his vassals and tributaries.

But in the year 990 AD disaster struck Sweyn Forkbeard. With a great fleet the Swedish King Eric the Victorious invaded Denmark and drove the son of Harald Gormsson from his realm. With his remaining followers Sweyn fled to the island of the Anglo-Saxons to devastate the counties and kingdoms of the Britons. He found refuge in the Danelaw and was soon accepted as the king of the Northmen there. When Sweyn Forkbeard retook his kingdom in the year 993 AD, he discovered that the Jomsvikings had become allies of the Polish king during his absence. Old Jarl Palnatoki had died and his successor Jarl Sigvaldi had been tricked into swearing fealty to the Polish King Mieszko. In secret the jarl of the Vikings of Pomerania remained friendly towards the Danish king.
The following year the Jomsvikings under Jarl Sigvaldi attempted to invade Trøndelag again for King Sweyn, and to settle their score. But again they were sorely defeated.

*